Praise for
A Date with the Fairy Drag Queen

"A sense of magic and wonder hovers over every page of Julie Turner's touching debut novel. Protagonist Saskia Nash takes us on a lyrical journey that bridges worlds: Europe and America; the past and present; the sacred and the human. Ultimately, it is an empowering story about how we meet the accidents in our life, some tragic, some for the better. In the deft hand of Turner, embodied by Saskia, the bitterest of pills can become the most delicate of sweets. Condemned for a fully human choice she makes, Saskia finds herself emotionally and literally banished from the world she knows, only to find another that holds more meaning and opportunity to give and receive empathy than she could've imagined. Like an alchemist turning iron into gold, Saskia transforms the unfair pain of life into a wondrous gift."

—Alfredo Botello, author of
Spin Cycle: Notes From A Reluctant Caregiver

"*A Date with the Fairy Drag Queen* follows Saskia Nash, a young woman caught between the legacies of two homelands—her mother's Germany and her father's America. Haunted by the loss of the mother she never knew, Saskia finds solace in myth and storytelling, using them as a bridge to her past and as a balm for the present. At a hospice for men living with and dying from AIDS, she discovers an unlikely family and the redemptive power of connection, compassion, and chosen kinship. Narrated in Saskia's intimate, searching voice, this poignant novel explores how we navigate grief, identity, and the fragile magic of human resilience. Lyrical, tender, and unforgettable, *A Date with the Fairy Drag Queen* is a story that lingers long after the final page."

—Patricia Smith, author of *The Year of Needy Girls*

"Julie Harthill Turner holds our hand as she leads us through Saskia's journey of loss, love, loss again, and triumph. This is the reason we write. This is the reason we read."

—Greg Smith, author of *The Agile Writer Method*

"An unlikely friendship flourishes in this beautiful story about family—of origin and chosen—and navigating the complicated emotional terrain of personal history, faith, and identity. Five stars!"

—Becca Ayers, Broadway performer

"What a powerful story. This short novel is brimming with meaning, lessons, and all the emotions. From the bitter disappointment in the church leader she trusted to the magic of selfless friendship, this story touches on so much of what it means to be human. Even if the reader can't personally identify with the Catholic Church, bisexuality, AIDS, or any of the other touching and poignant themes, the author manages to distill all of these into an exploration of the human experience. It's a compelling tale, but also one that is relevant for anyone who wants to feel connected to other humans, no matter their differences. My final takeaway is a message of unity and love."

—Carol Maloney Scott, author of *The Funeral Date*, *Nobody Tells Lia Anything*, and *There Are No Men*

"Turner's first name should be Page. From the first sentence to the last, *A Date with the Fairy Drag Queen* is a literary marvel, a riveting read, a guidebook to sexuality and identity, and a true work of art. This book offers representation and relatable romance while also capturing platonic love, partnership, and support. From disposable, disrespectful love to the last dance with chosen family, Turner's prose shines."

—Miranda Faye Dillon, award-winning author of *The Unshatterables*

"Julie Turner's *A Date with the Fairy Drag Queen* is a must-read for anyone who's been forced to repress, or silence, their authentic longings, their truest selves. Written with tenderness and verve, the story of Saskia Nash resonates with a potency that at first pulses within, but eventually, with the support of angels, both living and eternal, propels her emergence into a fully realized being living with authenticity, self-awareness, and a love that is both generous and self-affirming. A heartbreaking and heartwarming debut."

—David Hicks, author of *The Gospel According to Danny*

"Julie Turner's luminous, layered novel is both elegy and blessing. Through the lyrical voice of protagonist Saskia Nash, we join the sacred journey of a young woman haunted by the loss of the mother she never knew and suspended between two cultures—maternal and paternal.

"Scorned by the community that once claimed to offer grace, she experiences a devastating loss of choice. An unexpected twist brings us along with her to witness the redemptive power of queer resilience in the shadow of the AIDS crisis. This debut novel gives us a community full of love in a time of devastation—a space where chosen family and the magic of storytelling become sacrament."

—Rev. Dr. Brenda Walker, author of the forthcoming memoir *Martine: The Transgender Sister I Never Knew*

"The world would be a brighter place if more of us had a Wednesday night Magic Circle (Nutella included, of course). Julie Harthill Turner's *A Date with the Fairy Drag Queen* is a journey between cultures, continents, and traditions—a journey indeed full of magic where 'women are the secret keepers.' Through the voice of narrator Saskia, we are reminded that the power of a mother's love (and a strong feminist lineage) can succor us from beyond the grave; we learn that nothing leaves a more bitter aftertaste than the loss of choice; and we discover that redemption and grace often walk arm in arm. Saskia navigates a new country and a religion that betrays her, unwittingly steering for the least fairy-tale-like landing imaginable: a halfway house for men dying from AIDS. There, 'family' takes on a new meaning, and Saskia herself finds peace. If you're needing a booster

shot of faith in human nature, put this on top of your to-be-read pile!"
 —Joanna Lee, Poet Laureate of Richmond, Virginia, and author of *Dissections*

"This bold and touching exploration of belonging, created family, and identity is sure to resonate with anyone finding themselves starting over, uncertain about their future, and seeking connection."
 —Sassafras Patterdale (formerly Lowrey), author of *Lost Boi*, *Roving Pack*, and *Kicked Out*

"A beautiful, heartfelt tale of love and loss. You'll devour each page. "
 —Bill Konigsberg, award-winning author of *Openly Straight* and *Destination Unknown*

"Saskia's story is both unique and compelling and ultimately universal. 'Where do I belong?' is the human heart's constant cry, and Julie Turner deftly and gracefully guides us to the answer: beside each other."
 —Emily Carpenter, author of *Gothictown*

"Born in the shadow of loss and torn between two worlds,

Saskia Nash's life is a tapestry of magic, history, and identity. In her debut novel, Julie Harthill Turner brings to life Saskia's journey as the daughter of a fiercely independent German folklorist and an exuberant American historian. Struggling with questions of belonging, love, and legacy, Saskia wonders, *Am I a failure as a German daughter or a success as an American one?*

"Caught between her mother's belief in ancestral magic and her father's faith in America's promise, Saskia must reconcile her mother's haunting absence with her father's larger-than-life presence. Along the way, she faces the failings of the Catholic Church, accepts her bisexuality, and discovers her own voice amid the chaos. Guided by her grandfather's wisdom and magical moments from her heritage, Saskia navigates a world steeped in old-world mysticism and modern realities.

"With humor, heartbreak, and whimsy, *A Date with the Fairy Drag Queen* explores identity, family, and the enduring power of storytelling. For anyone who has felt torn between worlds or struggled to define themselves, this novel is a poignant reminder that our stories—both inherited and created—shape who we are."

—Cindy L Cunningham, PhD, founder of Wellspring Writing Collective and author of *Wild Woman: Memoir in Pieces*

"Heartbreaking in the first few chapters, then bittersweet and beautiful throughout, Julie Turner's not-a-memoir-yet-with-parts-drawn-from-life novel conveys raw emotion through her beautiful prose as main character Saskia works

personal tragedy by taking care of a dying man in 1990. Turner has an eye for detail that captures how someone can be beautiful even as they die of a horrible disease. An unusual and interesting read."
—Allison Ashton, author of *Sweet, Spicy, Delicate*

"A heartfelt tale filled with warmth, wisdom, and delightfully vivid characters."
—Marshall Thornton, Lambda award-winning author of *Femme* and *Father of the Bride*

A Date with the Fairy Drag Queen
by Julie Harthill Turner

© Copyright 2025 Julie Harthill Turner

ISBN 979-8-88824-742-6

All rights reserved. No part of this publication may be reproduced, stored in a retrieval system, or transmitted in any form or by any means—electronic, mechanical, photocopy, recording, or any other—except for brief quotations in printed reviews, without the prior written permission of the author.

This is a work of fiction. All the characters in this book are fictitious, and any resemblance to actual persons, living or dead, is purely coincidental. The names, incidents, dialogue, and opinions expressed are products of the author's imagination and are not to be construed as real.

Edited by Miranda Dillon
Cover design by Catherine Herold

Published by

◣ köehlerbooks™

3705 Shore Drive
Virginia Beach, VA 23455
800-435-4811
www.koehlerbooks.com

A Date with the Fairy Drag Queen

Julie Harthill Turner

VIRGINIA BEACH
CAPE CHARLES

To the misfits and outcasts, weirdos and eccentrics. May you have many Magic Circles in places where you feel at home.

To my given family, who choose to love me just as I am, "warts and all."

To my chosen family, which continues to grow day by day.

To Alex and Sebastian, who make it a joy to be a mom.
And to their children, Franklin and Oliver and Baby Girl on the way. Omi loves you to the moon and back.

And to David. When I got fired from my job, he told me I should use the extra time to finish my novel. "The End" is for you, my love.

CHAPTER 1

Early 1970s, Germany

MY MOTHER TOOK her last earthly breath as I took my first. It was 1970. Willy Brandt was the chancellor of Germany. Opa supported Herr Brandt, a champion for the people. Led Zeppelin's "Whole Lotta Love" was the number one hit in Germany. Opa and Papa agreed they preferred oompah bands and classical music. Papa, in his nostalgic retelling of my birth, told me that Petra Nash simply spoke me into being.

"Your mother was a storyteller," Papa said. "And you, my darling Saskia Nash, her greatest story." My father talked about her so much, I felt as though I knew her.

"She didn't fit the stoic, cold German mold," he said. "She belonged to the wild women, the storytellers, the witches, the women who hold up the sky." I often wondered what it meant that women "hold up the sky." I learned later that it was from a Chinese proverb—"Women hold up half the sky"—and it was a battle cry for women's emancipation.

"Your mother was a fierce advocate for women's rights," Papa explained. Papa told me many stories about my mother. I devoured them. "Even as an infant," Papa told me, "I'd soothe you to sleep with stories of your mama."

I loved the story of her kindergarten teacher trying to tame her spirit—my mother was muzzled when the teacher thought she was biting her classmates. They just didn't recognize the wolf-child at play.

"Boys were drawn to the fiery thick ginger locks she kept in braids," Papa explained. "Once, a young man, mesmerized by the braids in front of him, took his scissors as though in a trance and cut them off. He escaped with one, and she rescued the other. She kept her hair short for the rest of her life." My mother had kept the braid in a photo album. Papa would show it to me, and I'd marvel at the beautiful auburn hair. *I wish I inherited it from her.*

"Why did the boy cut off her hair?" I asked.

"Sometimes, that's the way boys show they like you. They tease or do something dramatic for attention," Papa said.

"Bullshit!" Petra had shouted at my father the first time she told him the story and he'd casually said the boy must have liked her. "If we ever have a daughter," she said to Papa, her index finger pointed right under his nose, "we are *not* teaching her that bullshit."

Papa was a history professor by training and a showman by nature. He delighted in walking into his university classrooms, standing dramatically on his desk, and bringing historical figures to life. He could conjure up Richard Wagner or Bobby Kennedy, Cleopatra and Mark Antony. With drama and flair, he could reenact a mob lynching or a soldier's last moments before his head was blown off by an enemy. With excruciating detail. So much, you could believe he himself had been the crucified Jesus. His students walked into all final exams to the sounds of Wagner's *"Die Walküre."*

Professor Jack Nash was dramatic. He was handsome and charismatic. And his intellect was immeasurable. His students hung on every word. The young men tried to emulate his style—bell-bottoms, turtleneck sweaters, and shaggy hair with bangs falling in their eyes. They discussed and reenacted famous speeches and talked about women's rights.

The young women swooned and seduced and paid extra attention to their hair and lipstick on the days they had class with Professor Nash. Each lecture was a performance, each performance a showstopper.

But when it came to talking about how my mom died, he would get a faraway look in his eyes, and he'd pat me on my head.

"She was working on her dissertation on folklore and narrative and would read sections aloud to you. That day she cradled her stomach with such tenderness, finished whispering the story of 'The Shoemaker and the Elves.'" His voice trailed off for a moment as he remembered. Papa looked deep into my eyes. "And then she just whispered you into being."

As I got older and gained knowledge about the birds and the bees, I'd ask, "Who cut the cord, Papa?"

He'd shake his head at my silliness. "No one, darling. That's how the stories live on. That's how her voice still speaks in you." He was a stickler for historical accuracy, eschewed magic, and the supernatural. But he never wavered on the myth he created around my birth. I don't think he could bear to think of her in pain. I stopped asking. Eventually, Opa told me what actually happened, but I loved Papa's version best. I would touch my belly button and feel the cord connecting me to her.

In Papa's reimagining, there is no skyrocketing blood pressure, no ambulance ride to the local *Krankenhaus*. There are no blazing hospital lights, no crimson-stained bed sheets smelling of vomit, sweat, and piss. There was no chaos, and the air wasn't tinged with desperation.

In his fairy-tale version of "the great birth," he doesn't faint when the *Krankenschwester*—nurse—hands him his blood-soaked daughter, insisting he cut the cord. Opa would tell me those things later.

My mother might have lived had she listened to the doctors in America telling her that an international flight in her condition would be too taxing. But Petra was adamant. She had the power of all the feminine beings in her ancestry coursing through her veins.

"My daughter will be born in Germany," she insisted. Papa pleaded with her to listen to reason.

"I will not have an American daughter," she vowed.

"But I'm American, darling," he stated. "So, she will at the very least have dual citizenship."

The glare from my mother told him that his flippant, practical response was not welcome.

In the end, they both got what they wanted. I was born in Germany, and I ended up as American as, well, all children torn between the ghost of their dead mother and the pull of their beloved father. Torn between two worlds.

I was ten during the "Miracle on Ice" at Lake Placid. Papa and I had been in the States—on the East Coast—for a few years, and we'd found a mutual love of hockey. I was only vaguely aware of the politics of the game, but I was rooting for the US against Russia with all my being. When we conquered the Soviets, the American flag was raised, and the anthem began, Papa and I clasped hands, sang along at the top of our lungs, and wept. I was identifying more and more as American. But I was devastated when Argentina beat West Germany in the 1986 World Cup.

I loved American television ads—my favorite commercial was the Coca-Cola "I'd Like to Buy the World a Coke." I thought that commercial was magical, which is exactly why my mother had so dreaded my growing up in America. I was enchanted by consumerism. Yet I longed for the 8 p.m. television cartoon—*Sandmännchen*—when the Sandman would invite all German children to go to sleep.

I was one-hundred-percent all-American. And German too. The kid who loved bologna and cheese sandwiches but couldn't stand peanut butter and pumpkin pie. I loved Halloween and hoarded all the Snickers bars I could. And I equally pined for a warm

German *Bretzel* with sweet butter and a walk in the Black Forest. As my German accent faded and my English became more "American," I would dream in German, feeling the tugging at my belly button and the whisper in my ear, "Don't forget who you are." I wondered if this was how a mutt felt from the SPCA. Part shepherd, part collie, all dog. Just never quite feeling like a purebred.

"I will not stay in the States to have this baby. She will be born where enchantment still exists." Petra believed all humans possessed magic. She was a folklorist who maintained that all ancient stories held deep truths. That all people had access to the mysteries and magic of the unseen world as long as they kept searching for it and their hearts didn't turn cynical. "Most Americans will never believe in, let alone access, their own magic," she opined. And she kept going, getting more passionate the more she argued with Jack.

"The isms all get in the way, Jack." She was fierce in her attack on consumerism. "Capitalism, fundamentalism, narcissism, ism, ism, ism." She'd rattle them off in a tirade against the land of the free. Of course, she benefited from that land: her job, which offered an excellent salary for a university professor on a green card, a handsome husband who doted on her, a break from her interfering father, independence. Yet when it came time to talk about giving birth, she wouldn't budge.

"You will risk orphaning your daughter for some make-believe fairy tales?" Papa was outraged and heartbroken. He held his young wife's hand in his own, knowing her will was stronger than any words he could conjure up to convince her with his prolific gift of tongue. It was how he'd first charmed the strong-willed, beautiful, wild creature in the hospital bed. My mom had been an exchange student at the university where my father was studying history. She was his German tutor. My father could persuade the sea to turn away from the shore. But my mother was Mount Olympus.

"Doctors don't know everything. They could be wrong. If they're right, Saskia will have my father, Otto. She'll have you. Your teaching job at the university is waiting for you." She didn't speak about the teaching job waiting for her at the same institution. I can picture my father pacing the hospital room, chewing on the nails on his right hand, taking deep sighs with a frown on his face. It's midwinter on the East Coast, and he's wearing bell-bottom plaid pants with a navy-blue turtleneck sweater and thick, horn rimmed glasses. His shoulder-length brown shag is in his face, and he keeps licking the mustache he thinks is groovy but looks like a caterpillar attacked him under his straight and delicate nose. He's thinking of just the right argument to convince her to take the recommended bed rest and delay the international travel until after my birth.

"And she will have the wisdom of the Motherland," my mother continued. "The smell of the forest, how to take a proper walk. She will be able to appreciate the finer things in life. I want her to explore old castle ruins and search the forest floors for mushrooms and moss, not shopping malls for jeans and tennis shoes." My father wanted to point out that there were finer things in America too. And German teenagers went crazy for American jeans and Nike tennis shoes. But he remained silent. He understood what his wife was trying to say. She'd explained it to him over and over again. In Germany things were simpler and more grounded. You could stand amid castle ruins and feel an ancestral connection.

"I want her to know *who* she is deep down," Petra continued, lost in her reverie.

"In America all she would learn is what others want her to be. In Germany she'll be connected to all the women who've come before her, standing on the shoulders of the ancestors whose blood pulses through her veins. She will discover who she was meant to be." Jack didn't interrupt. Petra was beautiful in her reverie. If he mentioned how she'd once been so desperate to leave Germany or suggested pregnancy brain was making her nostalgic for a place she had once abhorred, she'd turn angry and defensive.

"America," my mother said, "may be the land of opportunity, but it has lost its enchantment." Jack Nash had no argument left in him. What Petra believed about Germany, he felt fiercely about America. A land where new dreams could be forged, where truth lay yet to be discovered. Despite his passion for history, he believed in creating new stories, not recycling the old ones that had outlasted their usefulness. The old stories were there as lessons and to inform forward progress.

And so, despite doctors' warnings and her husband's pleas, they boarded the Lufthansa 747 and crossed the Atlantic so I could be born a proper German child.

"Your mother and I didn't fight much," Papa said. "But the fight in that hospital room was a real doozy." He would tell me years later that he thinks it was at that moment, while my mother lay close to death in a hospital bed, just around the corner from where she had herself been born, that I would inherit an inner turmoil that would plague me for many years. Caught between my mother's call back to her homeland and my father's vision of the future. So often, when I reflect back as an adult, I wonder, *Am I a failure as a German daughter or a success as an American one?*

CHAPTER 2

Early March 1990, East Coast, United States

I STARED AT "JESUS is watching you" scrawled into the bathroom stall door. I felt naked and exposed. And so sad. Dorm bathrooms weren't very different from high school bathrooms, except at a Catholic college, there were a few more "Don't get on your knees for a boy before you get on your knees for Jesus" than "Susie loves Johnny." They still smelled like shit and piss and blood and cherry Lip Smacker lip balm. A handful of girls walked in the bathroom, gossiping about a party the night before.

"Has anyone seen Saskia?" my roommate Lisa asked. "We're supposed to head to breakfast together." I lifted my feet from the bathroom floor in case Lisa decided to check under the stall. She'd recognize my fluffy purple cotton slippers.

"Nope, you sure she's not passed out somewhere?" I recognized but couldn't place the voice. Lisa laughed. They all knew I didn't drink much. Not with the threat of Papa finding out.

If only it had just been a blow job. If only Father Hamilton hadn't encouraged me to flirt with his favorite seminarian. If only I had listened when some other seminarians in class had insisted that girls shouldn't be in theology classes with men studying to be priests. My hand fumbled to get the stick positioned so my piss would hit it.

How many others had sat the agonizing five minutes waiting for the world to come crashing down? Either felt a rush of relief they'd dodged a bullet—free to carry on being reckless and carefree. Or felt the now-what pit-in-the-stomach dread. *How am I going to tell him? Will I keep it?* Thinking about the "or" curdled my stomach and churned its contents. I struggled to contain the gagging. Gagging reflex. What a laugh. I'd trade anything for the gagging reflex to be coming from a blow job. Not from one irresponsible moment of terrible lack of judgment.

◆◆◆

I've always wanted to be a mom. I think growing up without a mom made me ache for the possibility even more. I'd kept notes in my head of all the things I'd do with a little girl that I hadn't experienced with a mother of my own. Brushing her hair, wearing matching pajamas. Getting manis and pedis and giggling together. I envisioned myself in my early thirties with a husband and career. We'd both cry with joy at the pink plus sign.

"How will we tell everyone?" we'd ask while we dreamed of the perfect reveal. Or maybe with a wife and sperm donor. Our love strong enough to combat any hatred we'd encounter. No matter the who-with, my future always involved motherhood.

Papa used to throw lavish themed parties for his students and colleagues. On the poet Robert Burns's birthday, he'd dress in a kilt, prepare Haggis, and recite,

> *O my Luve is like a red, red rose,*
> *That's newly sprung in June:*
> *O my Luve is like the melody,*
> *That's sweetly played in tune.*

His Scottish accident was terrible. His charm, unquestionable.

While he entertained and enchanted, I took the younger children into the basement and reveled in their innocence. I was fascinated by the little boys who could take a chair and a blanket and turn it into a play fort. And was delighted by the little girls and their cries of "Let's pretend! Saskia, let's pretend I'm the doctor and you have a sore throat." And I'd open my mouth and say *ah*. And the child would shake their head and say, "Bad news, Saskia. You have prep throat." I loved the words the kids would mix up.

I soaked up their attention. I had a collection of children's books they could go through, and I'd read one after the other, never tiring of the repetition. I hadn't had a mother, but I had a maternal presence and a maternal instinct.

One year on New Year's Eve, Papa threw a party. The dean of students brought his wife and their little girl Maggie. Four-year-old Maggie was dressed in her snoopy pajamas, thumb in her mouth, head down. She had her arms around her dad's legs. It took a while for Maggie to warm up to me. When she did, she clung to me the rest of the evening, not leaving my side. When it came to bedtime, she sat in my lap and asked me to read. As I read *The Very Hungry Caterpillar*, she curled up against me, thumb still in her mouth, and sighed.

"My mommy doesn't love me," she said. She placed her head down on my shoulder and went to sleep. She smelled of baby powder and innocence. Little Maggie has always haunted me. How does a four-year-old come to believe their mommy doesn't love them? I couldn't imagine having anything but unconditional love for a child.

Allen and I had talked about marriage and children . . . once. A what-if-you-weren't-going-to-be-a-priest kind of talk.

"Could you picture yourself being married and having kids?" I asked. We were lying on the bed in my dorm listening to Jethro Tull discussing agape versus platonic love for our Christian Love and Marriage seminar.

"In theory, yes. I've always believed that in order to be a good spiritual father, you have to have the capacity to be a good earthly father." Allen ran his fingers through my hair and hummed along to "Sweet Dreams (Are Made of This)." Annie Lennox was an integral part of my college soundtrack.

"What about in reality?" I asked. "If we'd met before you were in seminary?"

"Don't be ridiculous, Saskia." He chuckled. "First of all, we'll never have sex. And if I did get married, I'd marry a virgin who grew up in the church." He looked over and caught me wiping my tears.

"Nothing personal, babe." He laughed. Even though I knew this was a hypothetical, fairy-tale conversation, it felt *very* personal.

"God would forbid me to marry a woman who'd acted on her unnatural impulses with another woman." Here it was. Spoken so nonchalantly. The truth hanging in the air between us. He'd have accepted my bisexuality "theoretically." If I'd kept it in the closet. It wouldn't matter if I never touched another woman again. I was impure.

◄◆►

Five minutes feels like purgatory when life hangs in the balance. With shaking, sweaty hands, I forced myself to look at the stick. Before I could reposition myself on the toilet, I vomited all over my lap. I missed classes the entire next week. Lisa hovered over me, worried I had the flu. Her attention was cloying, and each expression of concern made me feel like a fraud.

"For God's sake, Lisa," I snapped, "unless you can make my dead mother's homemade chicken noodle soup, you need to just leave me the fuck alone." I regretted my words as soon as they left my mouth. Lisa didn't have many friends, and she was only trying to be kind.

But I didn't want kindness. I wanted to wake up from my nightmare and pretend I'd never met Allen Tucker. Or be on the *Herrenstrasse* with Opa. Surely, he'd whisper the daffodils into bloom for me.

After a week of avoiding Allen, I knew I had to tell him. Though he probably suspected it already. We didn't use a condom. I wasn't on the pill. All it takes is one time. I don't think even he was entirely convinced by the "pullout" method of contraception. He had six siblings, after all.

Then we'd have a choice to make. Keep it or give it up. One choice would end his vocation. The other, giving up a baby after carrying it in my womb for nine months, would be my worst nightmare. Or so I thought.

We agreed to meet at Titan's Bar. I told him I had something important to tell him. I felt nauseated all over again as soon as I saw him. And he wasn't alone. Of course he wasn't. Father Hamilton was his puppeteer. I walked over to their table on legs that felt like spaghetti.

"We know why you're here," said Father Hamilton. I was startled.

"Your roommate found this in the trash. She's concerned about you." Father Hamilton pulled the EPT test from the pocket of his blazer. *Shit! She went through my trash!*

"We're also concerned about your health and spiritual well-being," Father Hamilton said and glanced at Allen. "But we have a sacred obligation to see Allen fulfill his spiritual destiny. He'll be a great priest. Maybe even bishop or cardinal someday. One mistake shouldn't cost him his future." I stared at the beloved priest in numb silence. Father Hamilton continued, "We've made arrangements for you to stay at Pippin House after your appointment." I looked at Allen, wanting him to look at me. But he just kept his head down. Father Hamilton placed a large, thick envelope in the middle of the table. The words "Planned Parenthood, $300" were scribbled in Father Hamilton's barely legible cursive. Not pro-life. Just pro making sure their golden boy had his life.

CHAPTER 3

Early 1970s, Germany

MY DEAD MOTHER loomed everywhere. Photographs of her hung throughout the apartment Papa and I shared with Opa. Some of the photographs hung crookedly on the walls. But Papa wouldn't change them, sure that Petra had moved them.

"She always teased me about my need to have everything just so," Papa explained. "If she wants her picture hung askew, so be it." Red-haired and freckle-faced, she was always smiling. Licking an ice-cream cone, hugging a tree, face covered in cake from my parents' wedding. She was radiant. And happy. In every photo. My favorite was the last photograph taken of her. She wore a simple black maternity dress and white go-go boots. She cradled her swollen belly with such tenderness. Looking at that photo, the love for her unborn child was obvious.

"You have your mother's nose, Saskia," Papa told me. "And her laugh. That laugh, one of the most beautiful sounds I've heard." For a long time, I thought that Papa had something wrong with his eyes. They were always leaking. I had my mother's nose and laugh but inherited Papa's tender heart.

Our apartment was on the second story above Magdalena's,

the flower shop Opa owned. It was the best smelling apartment building in the city—the waft of floral in the air and the smell of strong coffee brewing. Except for maybe the *Bäckerei*—bakery—around the corner. The smell of fresh bread and apple streusel was lovely too. The three-bedroom apartment was spacious and warm. Bookshelves lined the walls, bursting at the seams with books as varied as the flowers in the shop. Thomas Mann nestled next to Martin Heidegger. Encyclopedias of botany intermingled with *The Complete Works of William Shakespeare*. The bottom shelf of the bookcase in my bedroom was piled with children's books and comics. *Grimms Märchen* and *Max und Moritz*. I spent hours immersed in those books.

But my favorite spot was the kitchen. Small and crowded with a china cabinet, a tiny dishwasher, and shelves holding mugs and various snacks—pretzel sticks were my favorite—the kitchen was our hub. If I sat quietly on the tall green stool, Opa would give me pretzel sticks and let me help cut the chives for the chicken noodle soup.

The kitchen was the most important place in the apartment. All the important decisions were made there: what we'd have for dinner, where we would take our next adventure, if I really had to go to bed at 8 p.m. It was the spot where the three of us spent most of our shared time together, Opa smoking his cigarettes and Papa preparing for his lessons.

It is also where we shared our Magic Circle. Once a week, on Wednesday evenings, we would gather in the kitchen for our special ritual. We would take our spots at the circular kitchen table. We each got a spoon and a mug of coffee. Nutella sat in the middle of the table. To this day, Nutella still tastes of safety and comfort. Opa would start by taking a heaping spoonful of chocolatey hazelnut paste and dipping it into his coffee. Then it was Papa's turn. Then mine. I would take as much Nutella as the spoon would hold, dunk it in the coffee, and then wait eagerly for the signal. Opa would drum his fingers on the table, look around to make sure we were all ready, and say, "Once we eat this magical potion, the circle will commence, and all things spoken will be valued and heard." Magic Circle was a time for us to express our hopes and fears, to share secrets, and to make plans. Papa wasn't allowed to bring work to the table, and on those Wednesdays, we'd have his undivided attention. During Magic Circle, I shared my darkest nightmares and my most grandiose dreams.

"I'll be an astronaut someday, fly a rocket to Mars," I promised. During Magic Circle, Papa and Opa weren't allowed to tell me this was impossible. There were some evenings when we didn't have any secrets to tell or plans to discuss or hopes and dreams to share. On those evenings, Opa would choose a book to read—*The Little Prince* was my favorite—or a new skill to teach me. It was during Magic Circle that I learned how to use a compass and protractor, to conjugate French verbs, and make the perfect soft-boiled egg. The kitchen was cozy, and our Magic Circle was safe. Until a Wednesday night shortly after my seventh birthday, when Papa broke the spell and turned our world upside down.

The photos of my mother fascinated me. Before I learned to crawl, Papa hung some of the photographs low to the ground so when I scooted on my tummy, I'd see her red curly hair and green eyes looking back at me.

"Your mama is so proud, Saskia," Papa would say. Or a picture would be high-chair level, facing me as I refused the peas being spooned in my direction.

"Take a big bite for your mama," he'd cajole and point to the photograph. "She's watching you."

"Oh, for Christ's sake," Opa would scold. "Just ask Saskia to eat a bite for her papa or for her opa. Petra is dead." Opa grabbed the spoon from Papa's hand, made a silly face, and effortlessly glided the peas into my mouth. I promptly spat them out. Papa and Opa were ill-equipped to care for a child on their own. But the apartment building was full of women who gave advice and pitched in. If it takes a village to raise a child, the tenants of the apartment on the *Herrenstrasse* were my tribe. Frau Trunst made sure I was being properly fed.

"Otto, Saskia needs more vegetables. I brought a carrot salad." She handed Opa the dish filled with her delicious salad. Whenever I wanted some, I would visit the second floor.

"Frau Trunst, Opa and Papa haven't given me any vegetables in a long time." Within hours, there'd be a new dish of salad, and Frau Trunst would scold the bachelors.

Frau Lehman loved to knit, and I was fascinated. I would visit her fourth-floor apartment and watch for hours. Her gnarled hands were a whirl of activity, and bright balls of yarn became a pair of socks or a sweater as if by magic. Frau Sturm's husband had died in World War II before they had any children. She never remarried. I was the closest she came to having a grandchild. I tried to avoid Frau Hirsch at any cost. She reeked of turnips and cigarettes and loved to pull on my ear lobe, which made me shiver.

Tall and thin, Frau Hirsch appeared frail, but I was terrified of her. She was full of advice for Opa and Papa, and most of that advice was aimed at reforming my behavior, putting me in my place, and trying to get me into dresses and hair bows.

"I can hear Saskia sing and laugh even next door," Frau Hirsch would scold. "You must teach her restraint. And no one can tell she's a girl with her short hair and pants." Opa and Papa just laughed at her. They weren't scared.

"That girl needs a mother," Frau Hirsch declared.

A village of six older German women, two bachelors, and an unladylike young girl—in the States, we could have made a sitcom.

"Your mother was overjoyed when she found out we were having a baby," Papa said. "She talked to you in the womb from the moment she knew." He paused, recalling his ephemeral wife and the way her arms tenderly cradled her growing stomach.

"She'd play Mozart in the background and regale you with her stories. Sometimes we'd go to the playground and sit on the swings together," he reminisced. "I loved to watch her hands on her growing belly, so protective of you and so very much in love."

These are not my own memories, of course, but I've heard the stories so often, I claim them as my own. And though my mother was physically dead, she pulsed through my veins, and the very same stories she'd told while she incubated me in her womb—her life waning in order to give me mine—lived in me and infused my dreams and daydreams.

A portrait of my mother as a teenager hung in the living room. She was holding a bouquet of daffodils and wearing a mysterious smile on her face.

"What secrets are you keeping, Mama?" I'd look in her eyes. And she winked at me. I was about four years old the first time she spoke to me.

"I'm always with you," she said. It felt like a soft tickle in my ear. "When you need me, just call for me." I loved that tickle in my ear—melodious and loving. Protective. At first, I only heard the voice if I was near the portrait. But as I grew older, I learned I could tune into it by quieting myself and imagining her eyes winking at me.

"What are you doing, Saskia?" Papa asked. I continued to stare, then turned to answer.

"I was talking to Mama," I said.

"Ah, Saskia. You know she's not real, don't you? Maybe I should find a wife," Papa said. He was afraid of what he'd created in me: an unnatural attachment to a dead woman I'd never known. "Are you happy, Saskia?" he said wistfully. Not so much a question directed at me but a dread in his heart. He hadn't been able to keep Petra happy. Was he creating a similar fate for his daughter?

"All children with big imaginations have imaginary friends, Jack," Opa said.

"But she's not imaginary," I protested. I couldn't explain it, and years later, I still can't. But that voice was my mother, who gave me advice and told me stories. I learned to pay attention to that voice. Eventually, I'd learn the hard way what happened when I didn't heed her advice. Petra Nash was my gut instinct, my intuition. I didn't question if she was real any more than I questioned Opa being able to whisper daffodils into bloom in the winter. Some things can't be explained by logic. That doesn't make them any less real.

I didn't feel the lack of a mother. I had a larger-than-life mythological mother goddess whose lifeblood pulsed through me and gave me powers I'd yet to discover. I had a father who went to work every day at the university and would put me in a Boulder backpack to the delight of his adoring students who weren't used to seeing babies transported in anything other than strollers. There was no lack of attention and doting. And I had an opa who believed his granddaughter hung the moon.

I was raised by two men who adored me and the myriad women who adored them. For the first seven years of my life, I believed I was the queen of my own realm, with a father who brought dead philosophers to life for adoring undergraduates and a grandfather who commanded the natural world and transformed big exploding balls of helium and hydrogen into the stars I held in my hands at night.

◆◆◆

To me, he was simply Opa, but Otto Stein was a legend. People came from miles around—even from as far away as France and Switzerland—to visit Magdalena's. Of course, it had the usual roses of all varieties—altissimo and anemones, blumenschmidt and bolero, Clothilde and Dortmund. Lilies bloomed, and Lady's Slippers enticed customers whose noses would start to tickle from the aroma as soon as they walked in. The shop was a kaleidoscope of color and seemed to have a magnetic pull. Even the most unromantic young men would find themselves walking in the shop, suddenly knowing they needed to let their girl know how much they loved her. They'd leave the shop with a beautiful bouquet and words of wisdom from Otto.

"Fresh flowers once a week will make your wife more attentive in the bedroom," he'd say, grinning, knowing somewhere there was a happy woman, and he had gained a new weekly customer. They were drawn to the colors, and Otto's advice, but it was mainly those who were suffering an illness or heartbreak or depression who were drawn in. Some had heard of him from miles away. Others had no idea why they walked into a flower shop when their lives were so miserable. But whether knowing or not, they came to hear him whisper the daffodils into bloom.

Osterglocken—Easter Bells—my grandfather called them. They naturally appeared each year around Easter and bloomed for a very short time. The daffodils portended wealth and good fortune, promised spring and rebirth. I loved them with all my heart. To this day, daffodil yellow calms my heart and soothes my soul.

But people wouldn't just come for his daffodils in springtime.

"Herr Otto," they'd say on a bitterly cold winter day, with fog on their breaths and snowflakes dusting their heavy wool coats. "Jakob is lying in bed with a fever and crying out in his delirium." Opa would nod, express his deepest regret, and reply, "There must be something that can be done for a boy with such a lovely smile and such a love of arithmetic." He'd wander around the shop, stopping to inspect a daisy or a bunch of wild chamomiles. If I happened to be in the shop, he'd wink at me and say, "Saskia, what do you think this poor boy needs?"

I'd hop up and down with excitement. "The bells, the bells," I'd shout. He'd reply, "Yes, exactly right, some Osterglocken would bring good fortune." Opa would bend over a dirt-filled flowerpot, whisper a few words, then present his customer with three perfect daffodils. The next week, the customer would return, and Opa would inquire, "How is your son?"

"Fantastic! Just yesterday, Jakob won the school's arithmetic prize!"

"Opa, whisper me a daffodil," I'd sometimes demand.

He would shake his head and scold me. "Saskia, you must be careful with magic. It can't be demanded or used for the whims of a little girl wanting to be entertained. *Osterglocken* are lovely, to be sure, but they are also known as Narcissus." And he told me the story of Narcissus the God, whose love of himself—his vanity—caused his death.

"Vanity is dangerous. Beauty and magic must be treasured, not taken for granted. The Easter Bells are beautiful and bring luck and good fortune, but if we are vain or have ill-intention in our hearts, we can whisper forth a withered bulb that portends death and despair." I'd never seen a withered daffodil. I hoped I never would.

I loved Magdalena's. But as often as I begged Opa to tell me the origin of the shop's name, he refused. "Some things aren't meant to be known, Saskia," he said mysteriously.

Treasures abound among the roses, rhododendron, lilies, lilacs, sunflowers, snapdragons, gerbera, and gladiolus. Brightly colored butterflies for transformation, a fragile, blown-glass dragonfly for change and light. And in the corner with the dirt-filled pots waiting to be whispered into bloom, were my favorites, the hand-carved ladybugs. All sizes and shapes, I was delighted by the ladybugs. More good luck portents. All around were trinkets for luck, but I came to know it was my grandfather's hard work and dedication that created good fortune.

Each week I helped Opa sweep the shop. He'd inspect my handiwork, and if it met with his approval, I got to pick out one of those ladybugs. Opa would take out his brown leather notebook and Stabilo pencil and record the date and the item and write my name with a little note: "For a job well done." I learned the world was magical and kind and fair, and if you worked hard, you'd be rewarded for a job well done.

As much as I loved spending time with Opa in the flower shop, I relished it when Papa would take me to class. Papa's students played with me as though I was a doll and fought over who could babysit on weekends when Papa and Opa would go out to a bar or see a movie. In the 1974 college yearbook, there is a photograph of me—golden blond hair in pigtails—wearing a corduroy green dress and rainboots with ladybugs. Papa says I'd been unofficially adopted as the school mascot. He'd take his American students to East Berlin by bus during their semester abroad. I'd board the bus with them before they departed for their grand adventure. While the students were gathering and loading their suitcases into the underbelly of the bus, he would grab the microphone from the driver and turn on the tunes. Though I was speaking primarily German at home—another of Petra's demands—I knew all the English words to every

Carpenter's song and a great many of the words I picked up from those American students as they boarded the bus.

"Fuck, shit, damn, cocksucker, Papa!" The students would giggle as my dad threw up his hands.

"If I catch the bastard who is teaching my daughter this imbecilic vocabulary . . ." he'd threaten.

"Bastard, Papa?" He'd groan, realizing his mistake.

And then I would grab the microphone from him and sing along with Karen Carpenter. "Sing, sing a song, make it happy, to last the whole day long." The students would cheer. And Papa's demeanor would soften.

"I think she'll be a famous singer someday, don't you?" Once he'd taken roll and all the students were accounted for, he'd escort me off the bus and into Opa's care. I begged him to let me go on those trips with him. I would fill with envy at the time his students got to spend with him. But traveling to East Berlin was not a trip for four-year-olds.

Instead, Opa would take me on our own adventures. My favorite was to visit the very spot where the Easter Bunny prepared the chicken noodle soup that he'd once taught my mother to make. The same recipe Opa now used so he could pass on my mom's healing powers whenever I had a cold or fever. Opa had often told me about the time he met the Easter Bunny, the one who gave Mama the recipe for her chicken noodle soup.

"There is a place in the Schwartzwald called Hirschsprung," Opa said. "Legend has it that a knight from a nearby castle went on a hunt for deer in the Höllental valley. He spotted a magnificent stag—one whose rack would earn him the reputation as a formidable hunter—and chased after it. The stag was fast and agile and easily scrambled over the rocks along the river. The knight continued to chase him, determined to bring home the trophy. He thought he could win his true love's heart with such a feat of determination and courage. The stag, however, afraid of death, leaped over the gorge and escaped into the hillside."

"And then what happened, Opa?" I asked. He would scratch his head and hem and haw. "Please tell me," I begged.

"I'll do better than tell you, Saskia. I'll take you to the Hirschsprung and show you."

And so, on one of our trips—a diversion, really, to appease me since Papa was going on another student trip to Berlin—we drove to the Hirschsprung to uncover the story of how my mother got the Easter Bunny's chicken soup recipe. Never at a shortage for women willing to watch the flower shop, Opa and I started off on our trip. We drove through narrow canyons and heavy woods. Opa regaled me with his tales and kept my attention with promises.

"Saskia, the first one to spot the river will get five deutsche mark." I'd keep my eyes peeled out my window.

"River, Opa, I see the river." He would pull over and put coins into a coin purse he carried especially for me.

"What next, Opa? What do I look for now?" In this way, the drive would pass quickly, my attention on whatever treasure I was searching for. By the time we reached our destination, I'd have a collection of coins for souvenirs. As we approached the Hirschsprung, the sky darkened, and clouds hung low over the hilltops. Opa put his brights on in his Volkswagen as we drove through a thick fog. He pulled over just after a bend in the road, into a parking lot filled with cars, some with license plates from outside Germany.

"There it is, Saskia!" he cried. For a moment, I couldn't make out anything in the dense fog. I followed where his finger was pointing and made out an eight-foot-tall bronze stag.

"Wow," I said, enthralled. "But where is the Easter Bunny?"

"The Easter Bunny keeps himself hidden except to a few very, *very* special people. But you see all this fog around you?" he asked. I nodded. "It's not really fog," he said. "It's the steam from the chicken noodle soup the Easter Bunny prepares year-round to nourish hunters who get lost giving chase to the stag. Can you smell the soup?" he asked.

I stared wide-eyed and breathed in as hard as I could. "Yes, Opa, I smell the chicken noodle soup. It smells just like the soup you make for me," I said with delight.

"That's because, once, when your mama was about your age, we came here. She was as enchanted as you are. And out of nowhere, the Easter Bunny appeared. And he whispered to her the secret recipe for his soup." The fog rolled off the hills, and I pictured my mother receiving her gift from the Easter Bunny.

"Always pay attention, Saskia. Your mother was a very special young girl. She always had an eye for things that others couldn't see. She has passed that on to you. Keep your eyes open, and you will receive gifts such as these." My eyes and my heart were wide open. I had my opa and papa and the blood of my mother coursing through my veins.

―・・―

Opa was a mensch. A true gentleman and kind person. The first to visit a friend in the hospital and bring flowers. Always quick with a compliment and able to carry on conversations on a variety of subjects. He was always most versed in the subject his companion was the most passionate about. When he first read me Johanna Spyri's *Heidi*, I became obsessed. He brought home a cassette of songs inspired by the children's book. I wore out the book and the cassette. Opa would talk to me about the young orphan girl sent to live with her grandfather in a remote cottage in the Swiss Alps with as much seriousness as he discussed the Cold War or whether to have an espresso or café au lait with his afternoon dessert—usually a healthy slice of *pflaumenkuchen*. He relished his daily plum cake.

Each afternoon, Opa would close the shop for one hour and

come to the apartment above to eat lunch and take a nap. While Frau Lehman or Frau Sturm did the dishes, I helped brew the coffee. And when it came time to wake him, I took the responsibility with great seriousness. During the Heidi phase, I'd approach the couch in his study where he took his nap, gently tap him on the shoulder, and whisper, "I want to be able to run around like the goats do." It was my favorite line from the novel Opa had patiently read me several times.

"Then I must get up from my nap," Opa said, "so the little goat can go run about." We sat at the kitchen table on three-legged stools. While he finished his coffee, I'd dangle my legs impatiently, ready to walk with him down the stairs and back into Magdalena's.

Opa had plenty of women of a certain age who were grandmotherly toward me. Along with the women in our apartment building, there was Oma at the train station. I didn't know her real name, but she lived next door to the station, and when we visited, she gave me baked pretzels with sweet butter and let me hold the Steiff teddy bear that had once belonged to her son. Its name was Bear. I thought that was a silly name for a teddy bear. If it had been mine, I would have named it Twinkle or Heidi. But I played with Bear and ate my pretzel, licking the sweet butter from my lips, as Opa wooed Oma at the train station. On special occasions, I'd be allowed to have a *Kinder Cola*—caffeine-free Coke—and I'd savor every sip.

"Just don't tell Papa," Opa would caution. It was our secret.

We also visited Omi with the fish—a somewhat plastic-looking fuchsia-haired woman with a spectacular aquarium full of brightly colored exotic fish.

"Opa, she looks just like that one," I said, giggling and pointing to a bright magenta fish. Opa tried to hush me, his cheeks reddening. But the fish lady wasn't mad.

"That's a Magenta Dottyback," she said. "It's my favorite too." She'd sit me in front of the tank with a piece of bread spread with Nutella while the grown-ups talked about things I didn't really understand. But I liked visiting Omi on the market best. She lived behind the Marktplatz, and on market days, we would stop and pick up a bouquet of flowers to take to her. Then Opa would help her gather empty wine bottles and other recycling, and the three of us would take them to the compactor together and then do our shopping.

"Saskia, what should we get from the market today?" Opa would ask. I always begged for raspberries and strawberries. We'd inspect each apple and pick out four that were "just right." On Saturdays, the butchers came to the market. Butchers were my favorite, with their gifts of *schinken* to eat while Opa ordered his pigs feet, cow tongue, and blutwurst. I loved the market. Omi on the market would make her selections, Opa would pay for them, and we'd walk her back to her apartment. I didn't learn until later that these women were all widows, and Opa was helping them in some way or another. Years later, during college, on my last visit to Germany, Opa and I shared a bottle of wine, and he told me about my real oma. Magdalena. What I learned about her would have spared me so much heartache and confusion had I known sooner. But Opa had made a promise to her. And he'd kept it as long as he could.

Every moment with Opa was an adventure. He loved to tell tall tales. Driving through the Swiss Alps, we'd pass fields with brown cows, and he'd slow down so I could take a closer look. "Saskia, do you know what kind of cows they are?" he'd ask. We were learning about different types of animals in kindergarten, and I'd reply, "Holstein!" And he would throw his head back and laugh.

"What are they teaching you in that kindergarten? I ought to go and give them a piece of my mind." His eyes twinkled. "Those are the cows that make the chocolate milk." I knew it wasn't factually true, but I believed him. If he could whisper daffodils into bloom, then perhaps his brown cows did make chocolate milk.

Best of all, I loved trips with Opa to the planetarium. Opa was on the board of directors of the Astronomical Association. He had the key to the planetarium and would take me once a week to peek through the telescope at the moon. It was so close, I felt as though I could catch it in my hands. On our last trip to the planetarium, a night when the moon was full, Opa stood behind me as I peered through the telescope.

"Even when we are far away from each other, Saskia, remember we are looking at the same moon." I stared at that moon for what seemed like hours. It pulled at me. I looked over at Opa. Even then, nearing seven years old, I could sense emotions from just the most subtle of signs. Sometimes, it was a smile not quite as wide as normal. Or a finger drumming on a knee just a bit quicker than usual. Today, I looked over and noticed that Opa had mismatched the buttons on his gray cardigan sweater, leaving an extra buttonhole at the bottom.

"Opa, there's no need to be sad," I said. "We won't ever be far away from each other." Just then, the moon dipped beneath cloud cover, and a shiver ran through me. I squeezed his hand tight, and we turned away from the telescope and started the walk back down the hill.

"Let it be so, Saskia. Let it be so."

CHAPTER 4

Early 1990s, East Coast, United States

THE ROOM SPUN, though I hadn't touched the Sam Adams Father Hamilton put in front of me. Father Hamilton's proclivity to order alcohol for even his underage students was part of his popularity. The staff at Titan's Bar turned a blind eye. *Nice touch. Pregnant women shouldn't drink. Unless they're going to get the fetus aborted at the insistence of their priest. Drink away, my child; it'll numb your pain.*

"So, all the time we spent during RCIA arguing about the church's position on abortion and your insistence that I couldn't be Catholic and pro-choice at the same time?" I stared at Father Hamilton in his roman collar. *Did he believe any of it? Or was his service to God actually an addiction to power and control clothed in fancy cassocks?*

"You know, mortal sin and automatic excommunication for those who procure it? Do you actually believe that?" I choked out. Tears flowed down my face, but I didn't care. "And it's my decision anyway. I get to choose whether or not to keep this baby. And Allen should get a say too." Allen didn't move except for the wringing of his hands. More and more, he was just a puppet, and Father Hamilton was the puppeteer.

"Allen's future is in the priesthood. God has made that very clear." *To whom?*

"What if my future is being a mom?" I whispered. I can hear his scornful laugh to this day.

"And give up your dreams of going into the Peace Corps, pursuing your Master of Divinity, and becoming a writer? You don't want to give all that up to raise a child on your own. And you can still be a mom after you've lived life a little." Anger and despair and sorrow roiled in me.

"I could give the baby up for adoption. Closed adoption. I wouldn't tell anyone who the father is, and there would be no way he could ever find out." I realized as I was talking that *I knew*. I wrapped my hands around the locket hanging from my neck. "Mama, it would have been a boy," I whispered. I also knew I wouldn't have the courage to defy Father Hamilton. I knew my argument was hollow to him. There would always be ways that Allen could be found out. It was in his best interest for the problem and the cause—me—to be out of the way.

At twenty, I sometimes felt so grown up, but in fact, I was still a child in many ways. A child who'd never had a full-time job, who didn't know how to balance a checkbook. Who had been a babysitter but never cared for a baby twenty-four hours a day. I couldn't handle a baby by myself. I felt lonelier than I'd ever known. If Allen had any feelings on the situation, I'd never know. His path had been forged for him. And that path didn't include me—and certainly not a child.

"And, as I recall," Father Hamilton said, "you were very vocal in our classes about being pro-choice. I think your specific words were 'I'd definitely consider an abortion if I got pregnant while I was in college.'" His condescension was so thick, you could cut it like melted butter. "Now, all of a sudden, you're getting high and mighty with me?" His voice was menacing. "This is not about you, darling Saskia. This is about a young man's future." *And God forbid I ruin that future.* The threat was clear. Don't interfere with the church.

"We were having a theoretical discussion about an area of church law I struggle with," I yelled. Allen looked at me in horror.

"Keep your fucking voice down," he hissed. *He does have a pulse.*

"A theoretical, abstract, hypothetical pregnancy. Not an actual human life. I theoretically believe in the death penalty too, but that doesn't mean I want to be the executioner." I was tired, distraught, and grasping at straws. "Pro-choice doesn't mean pro-abortion, you know." I felt as if the wind had been sucked out of me. Just like that, I had no fight left to give. But Father Hamilton wouldn't let up.

"Not only would it ruin any possibility of a career for you but think about your dad. What about his reputation? Are you willing to ruin his life too?" Papa. All this time, it hadn't occurred to me how much this would impact him. His status on campus. The pride he had in me. Straight-A student, active, and well-liked on campus. My success had an impact on him. Having a daughter pregnant by a seminarian would be devastating. I longed for Nutella and coffee. For that green stool in the old apartment. For Opa and our Magic Circle. But Magic Circle was just a silly tradition. For children. And I was no longer a child.

I glanced at the envelope. Father Hamilton noticed and picked it up.

"I'll take this for safekeeping. I'll give it to you when I drop you off for your appointment." His plan was in place.

"Why Pippin House?" I managed to ask.

What the hell is happening? Why don't I get to decide? I looked at Allen, his eyes focused on the menu he'd been reading for ten minutes. *What is it that you want?* I wanted him to look at me and show some emotion, some sign he had an independent thought about his baby.

"As you know, we've had a hard time placing a volunteer there, and you can do your community service immersion semester a year early. You have enough credits." I instinctively placed my hand on my stomach then quickly withdrew it. I shouldn't think of there being anything in my womb to protect. Father Hamilton had clearly thought long and hard about what to do about my problem. As the student coordinator for the campus volunteer program, I was well aware that Pippin House was the one organization that we hadn't been able to place anyone in. It was a home for "men living with AIDS," the brochure described.

"We like to encourage the men to focus on spending their last few months and days on living in the moment, not focused on the fact of their dying," Lester Douglas had told me in our initial intake interview for the student/organization matching program. Lester and his partner founded Pippin House when they were both home health nurses. They saw a horrible lack of care for their gay male friends dying of the horrific disease. "Pippin House. You know, from the musical? We wanted to help these men find their corner of the sky."

My mind was a flurry of tumbling thoughts hurdling at me faster than I could process them. *What is happening to me? How could I let this happen? Why is God punishing me?*

"And what about Holy Week?" Logical, analytical Saskia was taking over. Set emotion aside and worry about the details. I had a flute solo on Easter Sunday, and I was receiving the Rite for Christian Initiation for Adults (RCIA)—baptism, communion, and confirmation—at the Easter Vigil. I looked over at Allen again. Still no eye contact.

"Do you have anything to say, you fucking coward?" I screamed. "Do you have an opinion or thought about what to do about your fucking sperm donation?"

As soon as the rage escaped and the steam left my body, I collapsed into a torrent of tears.

"It's for the best," he said.

And so, the arrangements were made for me. As hard as I tried, I couldn't tap into my mother's energy or call upon the spirits. No wellspring of power flowed through me and gave me a voice.

It was as if the fetus temporarily renting space in my body had robbed me of my will to act on my behalf. And so, I became a robot, occasionally nodding in response to Father Hamilton's directions, sometimes muttering a quiet "yes," always acquiescing. *Because it was for the best, wasn't it? Allen deserved a chance to become a priest and maybe even a bishop or cardinal, didn't he? And at twenty, I didn't need to be saddled with a baby. Yes, I'd always wanted to be a mother. But not like this. And Father Hamilton, he's looking out for my best interest too. Right?*

"So, you want me to wait to have, um, to go to the... appointment until after Easter?" I asked. Another two weeks of agony. Morning sickness and pretending it was just something I ate. Avoiding Papa on campus because he'd know something wasn't right. Trying to avoid being in the dorm room at the same time as Lisa. I know she was just concerned when she went to Father Hamilton. But she also knew I was pregnant and would ask questions. And what would I say? "Hey, Father Hamilton is going to drive me to Planned Parenthood the day after Easter for my abortion. It's no biggie. He's going to hear my confession on Holy Thursday. I'll be absolved of any sin." Father Hamilton was one of the most idolized priests on campus, and no one worshipped him more than my roommate, a cradle Catholic who'd die if she knew I was getting an abortion and, worse, might lose her faith altogether if she knew that Father Hamilton was taking care of it.

The first time I met Father Hamilton was at Sunday night Mass in my dorm. It was the first week of classes, and there was a buzz about "Father What-A-Waste," the handsome, charismatic guitar-playing young priest who favored rock 'n' roll tunes over traditional hymns during services. You were more likely to hear Eric Clapton at Father Hamilton's Mass than "On Eagles Wings."

"You've gotta come to Mass at the dorm," older students were advising the freshman. "Father H is the BEST." Followed by giggles. And he was mesmerizing. If he hadn't been a priest, he'd have made a fantastic politician. *Or snake oil salesman.* The thought seemed to come out of nowhere. Though the way my locket burned against my skin, I knew better. Mama. He was the kind who looked you straight in the eye and made you believe you were the only person in the room. I gathered up my nerves and went to introduce myself before that first Mass, both proud and slightly embarrassed by my connection to the wildly popular history professor.

"Father Hamilton?" I stood and looked into his piercing blue eyes. He brushed away the bangs covering his forehead and reached for my hands, covering them with both of his. His gaze was so direct that I felt flush and looked away.

"New freshman?" he asked.

"I'm Professor Jack Nash's daughter," I said, starting to feel uncomfortable with his hands still in mine.

"Ah, we meet at last. You have a very adoring father. But you should introduce yourself as Saskia Nash. Our God calls us each by name. Look it up, Isaiah 43:1, my favorite Bible verse. You may be Jack's daughter, but more importantly, you are God's special creation." I managed to get my hands away from his and back away.

"Nice to meet you," I mumbled. I wanted to crawl away and never have him notice me again. *Be wary of that one, Saskia.* I clasped the locket around my neck and reminded myself to listen to my gut. The common room in the dorm was packed for the evening Mass. I felt a strange chill as I snuck out of the room, back toward my dorm, as Father Hamilton opened the service by singing Peter Simon's "Slip Slidin' Away" while strumming his guitar. Seeing the crowd fixated on the man in front of them, he resembled more of a cult figure than a Catholic priest. A rock star, not a man of God.

CHAPTER 5

Early 1970s, Germany

MAYBE IF I'D been paying more attention, I'd have noticed the shift. I would have been prepared for the news that would make the walls of my fairy-tale childhood come crumbling down. Opa's cardigans were more often misbuttoned than not. His normal daily routine became sporadic. Sometimes he wouldn't take a nap or would work in the flower shop through lunch.

Papa spent less time at the university and more time at home during the day. He'd leave in the evenings and come home well after Opa had put me to bed. Papa's moods grew darker, more melancholy. I'd beg him to tell me one of my mother's stories, and he'd shoo me away. "Fairy tales, Saskia, silly fairy tales. It's time you got that nonsense out of your head." He started taking down pictures of Mama. He didn't replace them, just left empty space hanging on the wall.

Sometimes he'd sneak into the apartment in the early morning only to find that Opa and I were already at the breakfast table eating soft-boiled eggs and drinking coffee, mine always 80 percent milk with a splash of coffee.

Soon, there were no more photographs of Mama. With the

absence, he began reminiscing about life in the East Coast, United States: Fourth of July fireworks, Thanksgiving Day parades, going to New England Patriot games, grocery stores that stayed open twenty-four hours a day.

"You'd like it, Saskia," he said.

"Well maybe someday you'll take me to visit," I replied. I got no response. He wasn't thinking about visits. His thoughts were far more permanent. Opa responded to Papa's reveries about America with a vehemence completely out of character. Sometimes their arguments would wake me up after I'd gone to bed, and I'd sneak just outside the kitchen to listen in.

"What is so great about America?" my grandfather roared. "It killed my daughter, yet you dare even suggest that you might leave with my only grandchild." The kitchen table was strewn with empty wine bottles and Brandy snifters with just a splash of amber left on the bottom. Opa's face was the color of beets, and Papa's hair was unkempt from running his hands through it in frustration.

"America didn't kill your daughter, you bastard," Papa hissed. "She killed herself for some fucked-up notion that raising our daughter in the US would have somehow ruined her." The ashtray was overflowing with cigarette stubs. My eyes burned from the smoke wafting out of the kitchen.

"And as a foreigner, I can't take my career any further here," Papa added.

"Ha! Exactly what Petra said to me when she left Germany," Opa said. "'Vati, there's no career for me here in Germany. America is where my studies can flourish,' she told me."

Opa's rage had simmered down, and he sat with his head in his hands.

"Everyone I love deserts me," he lamented. "I thought I had more time with Saskia.

"It's not Mars, Otto. And nothing is set in stone," Papa's tone had softened. I heard him say, "Nothing is set in stone," but I didn't believe it. Papa's heart had been back in America for a while now. They brought their fight to a détente, but my thoughts whirled in my head. *What would happen to Magic Circle? Would there be daffodils in America? What if I couldn't hear Mama anymore? Who would take care of Opa?* I turned toward my room to go back to bed, but instead I curled up on the green couch underneath the portrait of my mother.

CHAPTER 6

1990, East Coast, United States

"MS. NASH, YOU will be Catholic before you leave this institution," predicted Father Benedict, the only Franciscan priest on campus. It was the first day of Religion and the Human Quest taught by Father Benedict and Rabbi Steinberg. We were introducing ourselves: tell us your name, where you're from, and something interesting about yourself. All I could think of was that I played the flute. I suspected most people already knew I was Dr. Nash's daughter.

"I've played since I was nine years old, so I guess I'm looking for a group I can play with," I said.

"We'd love to have you play with the choir at Mass," Father Benedict said. Startled by my outburst of laughter, Father Benedict made his bold prediction.

"But I'm an atheist," I proclaimed, even though I still hadn't figured out what I really was. I knew, though, that I didn't believe in an old White man in the sky.

"An atheist who needs a place to play her flute," Father Benedict retorted.

And I did go to Mass and play my flute in the choir. The very first week of my freshman year. And never looked back. I signed up for all the religious studies classes I could. And before the end of my first semester, I approached Father Benedict.

"How do I convert to Catholicism?" I asked. This time, it was Father Benedict's time to burst out laughing. "The Jesuits suck you in every time," he said. "Take the RCIA classes with Father Hamilton. Call campus ministry, and they can give you all the information."

"RCIA?" I asked.

"Rite of Christian Initiation for Adults."

By the time I got off the phone with campus ministry, I had signed up to be a volunteer. I went to daily Mass and choir rehearsals on Thursday nights, played my flute at Sunday Mass, and attended a six-week catechism course with six other women wanting to become Catholic.

"So do we get a prize at the end of the class?" I joked.

Father Hamilton chuckled. "You get to choose whether you want to become fully Catholic. During Holy Week each year, the adults who convert go through the RCIA. You get baptized, take first communion, and are confirmed at the Easter Vigil."

"Sold!" I proclaimed. Maybe it was my competitive spirit, but I couldn't help thinking that I'd beaten Father Benedict's prediction. Catholic before the end of my first year of college.

"What's a girl doing in this class?" All eyes turned to me. I blushed. For weeks, Mike Donohue asked that same question every day at the beginning of class. Some days, I'd walk in and "No Girls Allowed" would be scrawled on the chalkboard.

"There is simply no point to a girl being in class with the seminarians. She's a distraction, and what's her motivation?" Mike argued. "She can't ever be a priest, after all." Mike Donohue was a man of misguided convictions. But at least I knew where he stood. Most of the rest of the guys were either overly polite, too formal, or simply ignored me, refusing any eye contact.

"You do know that this is a required course for a degree in religious studies, don't you?" I asked Mike.

"Perhaps it should tell you something that you are the first and only female religious studies major," he responded.

"I'm a trailblazer," I retorted.

"You're a fraud. College women are just looking for husbands, and you won't find one here. Rigorous theological examination is the domain of men, which is why we leave the more . . . domestic pursuits to you." I let Mike Donohue get the last word in. It wasn't worth my time to respond. Professor Roberts, our instructor for Contemplative Prayer, would give Mike a stern look but never correct him. The rest of the students—seminarians from the local seminary fulfilling their educational requirements—laughed awkwardly or were silent. *What am I doing here? The guys don't want me here. But I have every right to be here. Don't I?*

"Of course you do, my daughter. Your place is anywhere you want to be." It was an almost inaudible whisper, but Mama was there.

"Some of the great contemplatives were women." It was about three weeks into class, and I was fed up with Mike's bullying.

"I assume if Teresa of Ávila had walked into a classroom, you'd have ridiculed her too?" I challenged. My blood was boiling. Because I was female and would never be able to be a Catholic priest, these young men—I suspected it wasn't just Mike—considered me inferior.

"Have you read *The Interior Castle*?" I admonished. Their expressions told me they were not familiar with Teresa of Ávila's autobiography. I silently thanked Father Hamilton for lending me a copy as I was discerning who to choose as my patron saint for confirmation.

"Apparently, you are all dwarfs," I said. Then I recited from memory, "You must not build upon foundations of prayer and contemplation alone, for, unless you strive after the virtues and practice them, you will never grow to be more than dwarfs." I could feel my face flush. My hands and voice were shaking, but I could feel Mama giving me the courage of conviction. She would want me to make noise and take up space.

"You all may think I'm out of place here," I continued. "You may think that women don't belong in the classrooms with serious seminary students training for a life in service of God." I could see Professor Roberts nodding, encouraging me. "But I didn't sign up to learn with a bunch of intimidated young boys scared to stack up their intellects against a girl. I may not have a penis, but neither am I a dwarf." I took a deep breath and then continued, "And what about Hildegard of Bingen? Any of you familiar with her? You know, composer, philosopher, poet, mystic. She did not have a penis." I stopped speaking and sank back into my chair, exhausted and exhilarated.

Silence really is deafening. My heart was pounding as I finished my speech. I felt as though I'd channeled St. Teresa. I knew at that moment that she would be my patron. That she was the patron saint of headache sufferers seemed appropriate. Mike Donohue was one headache I was ready to get rid of.

And then Mike started to clap. And the others followed. I sat stunned for a minute, then stood up and curtsied. They laughed.

"Boys, she may not have a penis, but she has a brain," Mike said. "Okay, girlie, bring it." He winked at me. And with that, his bullying turned to teasing, and I became "one of the guys."

"Want to be my prayer partner?" Allen leaned over and asked me. We had an upcoming assignment to partner up and give a presentation on a form of prayer.

"If you think you can handle it," I responded. And grinned.

"Well, I do know about St. Hildegard and her 'visions.'" Allen replied. Hildegard of Bingen was said to have visions unlike any other—not apparitions or trances but sights she saw while fully awake. They became known as the "shadows of the living light." He winked at me. And I fell just a little bit in love with the man who could have talked circles around me on the lives of the saints but chose instead to let me have my shining moment.

"We're not supposed to be alone with a girl," Allen said. "We'll have to meet someplace public to work on our presentations." He seemed a bit embarrassed.

"So how are you supposed to learn to control yourself in the face of temptation?" I teased. "I mean, you are going to have to have one-on-one interactions with members of the fairer sex."

He laughed. "Well, they want us to get through seminary at least somewhat unscathed, I suppose."

"Are you allowed to flirt?" I wasn't sure where my boldness was coming from. "I mean, assuming that you'd want to flirt, um, sorry—" I stumbled over my words.

"Let's meet in the library. The librarian will make sure we keep our hands to ourselves and our flirting to a whisper," Allen said. I giggled. *What the hell are you doing, Saskia?* The thought matched the sense of unease I felt in my stomach.

I ignored the uneasy feeling and went tumbling head over heels. Despite all the obvious flirtation, Allen was the model of clerical restraint. We met in the library in a conference room enclosed in all glass. Occasionally, another seminarian would stroll by, and Allen would wave his hands as if to say "no monkey business going on here." The guys watched out for each other. I envied them sometimes.

"I'm flattered they think you'd be tempted by me," I teased. Allen blushed.

"Maybe they already know that I am," he said. "We know everything about each other and don't hide even the lustful thoughts in our heart." I grinned. "So, you have lustful thoughts about me?" *If you knew the lustful thoughts I have about you.*

"That's between me and the guys. What I do have thoughts

about is how we're going to do our presentation on prayer." Always practical. That was Allen. We worked on our presentation. Endlessly. We were using a method of prayer that involved turning to a random page in the Bible and blindly pointing a finger on a verse. Whatever text we landed on was our topic for contemplative prayer. Each time was different, so we practiced how we would demonstrate, who would do the talking, and what we would offer as the benefits for this type of prayer.

"I was impressed with your knowledge of saints," Allen said.

"All two of them." I laughed. "It just happened that I was studying them for RCIA, trying to decide who I want to choose for my patron saint for confirmation. I'm leaning toward St. Teresa." Allen was an encyclopedia of knowledge. "St. Drago is the patron saint of unattractive people," he recited. "St. Adrian of Nicomedia, the patron of arms dealers. Before his conversion, he used to persecute Christians. And then there's St. Friard d'Indret, the patron against wasps, who was said to have sent swarms of them after his tormentors."

I yawned and quickly covered my mouth. "It's not you or your stories. I'm just exhausted from an all-nighter last night preparing for my psychology lab exam," I apologized.

"Well then, pray to St. Dymphna, the patroness of crazy people and sleeping problems," he said. "Not that you're crazy." He was an endless wealth of knowledge. His deep brown eyes lit up when he got to talking about all things Catholic. *Damn, he'll make a good priest.*

"I should have come to you while I was discerning," I said. "I'm inspired by Teresa, of course, but I partly opted for her because I don't have a middle name, and I thought Saskia Teresa Nash sounded lovely." I was embarrassed to admit my flimsy reasoning for picking my patroness. It was like choosing a football team based on which one had the cutest quarterback.

"Do you have a confirmation sponsor?" Allen asked. Father Hamilton had mentioned we needed a sponsor.

"I haven't chosen one yet," I admitted.

"Well, now you have one," he said, "if you'd like for me to be, that is."

"Wow, really? Are you allowed to sponsor someone?" I asked. "And what is the purpose of the sponsor?"

"The primary responsibility of the sponsor is to provide the candidate prayerful support and guidance in his or her Christian walk and to take care that the confirmed person behaves as a true witness of Christ and faithfully fulfills the obligations inherent in this sacrament."

"You've been thinking about this for a while?" I grinned.

"Yep, I was hoping you'd agree. And that is from the Code of Canon Law. Number 892." I couldn't decide which I found more appealing, his physical attractiveness or his sharp mind. It didn't occur to me then that he sounded like a robot. And so, we prepared for confirmation and for our prayer presentation. We kept our hands to ourselves, though it was difficult for me. I wanted to touch him, hold his hand, kiss him. If he was experiencing temptation of the same nature, he kept it well hidden. I both admired and resented his restraint.

"Let's take a walk," Allen said. His invitation took me by surprise. We'd been meeting in the library for a few weeks now. Always in the glass bowl conference room, always with a seminarian or two walking by every half-hour.

"I want to show you my favorite spot on campus," he said. "I can't show you around the seminary, for obvious reasons, but the campus here has some beautiful spots." We headed from the library toward Main Hall. It was dusk, and the automatic lamps hadn't yet come on. *This could be romantic in other circumstances.*

"I've spent so much time here, I guess I take it for granted." I told Allen about moving to the States when I was seven so my dad could take a job at the university. "I practically grew up here," I continued. "I hated being at home with my nanny, Helga, so I spent as much time here as I possibly could. When it came time to pick a college, this was a no-brainer. I've wondered sometimes if it might have been better to go away, but I couldn't pass up the free tuition."

"So that's how an atheist ended up at a Jesuit institution." Allen laughed.

"That's how that atheist got roped into playing her flute for Mass and got brainwashed, um, converted." But, of course, it wasn't all about having a place to play the flute.

"I grew up in a diocesan Catholic Church in Minnesota," Allen said. "A very strict upbringing that is still ingrained in me. The Jesuits are too progressive in their views for my taste, but I am broadening my horizons, if not challenging my beliefs." We walked and talked for a few minutes. As we rounded the corner behind Main Hall, Allen stopped me.

"This is it. My favorite place on campus." We had stumbled onto a small grotto almost hidden in a patch of bushes. I thought I knew the campus like the back of my hand. But I'd never seen it before. Inside sat two stone benches on either side of a statue of the Virgin Mary. The statue was simply adorned, beautiful in its simplicity. What was most gripping, though, were the tears running down her face. I ran my fingers along her face and felt the moisture on my hands. I sat down on one of the benches.

"I like to think she's weeping for all the unborn children. I come here to pray for life," Allen said. Allen sat down next to me. I tensed.

I didn't want to ruin the mood and commented, "That's probably a discussion better left for another time." I knew we'd never see eye to eye. I wouldn't necessarily choose to have an abortion, but I vigorously supported a woman's right to choose.

"Well, she's also the patron of all humanity. I think that's pretty all-encompassing," he said.

"No wonder she's weeping then," I replied.

What do you weep for, Mother Mary? It can't just be for unborn children. Do you weep for those who are starving and orphaned and trafficked? For those who feel unloved and unsafe? Do you weep because I'm bisexual? Or do you just love all humanity so much that you weep when we have hatred in our hearts for those who are different from us?

"What made you decide to convert?" Allen asked. His question startled me out of my reverie. It was a question I'd been asking myself a lot recently.

"It's not something I can really explain," I said, clutching my locket. "I feel like I've been chasing something my whole life. I think, in Germany, I experienced God in everything around me, though I wouldn't have named it that. My mom died in childbirth, but I never had a chance to miss her because she was everywhere I looked. Her photograph, the kindergarten she attended. I learned to walk at the Schloss—the castle—where she learned to walk."

Mother Mary wasn't the only one weeping at this point. "I'm sorry to get so emotional. But we moved to the States, and I couldn't see her anywhere. My dad didn't hang any pictures of her. I think I latched on to any kid with a mom who showed interest in me. Often, that meant they dragged me along to church. I wanted that belonging. I found it here when I started playing the flute at Mass."

"I'm so sorry about your mom, Saskia," Allen said. I unclasped my locket and handed it to him. He opened it and stared at me. "You look just like her," he said.

"Yep, I've been told. I have her nose, her laugh, her spirit." He reached over to place the locket back around my neck. His fingers lingered a moment longer than was proper. Yet not long enough. "I used to hear her all the time in Germany. She spoke to me just as you and I are having a conversation. She still does, sometimes, but I've just gotten used to not listening for her guidance." To break up the mood, I said, "Right now, she's telling me to steer clear of the handsome seminarian who has stolen my heart."

Allen laughed. "Let me walk you back to your dorm. It's getting late, and we've got a presentation to give tomorrow." We strolled back to my dorm. He opened the front door for me and then hugged me goodbye. His embrace excited and repulsed me. I felt a shiver as he walked toward the parking lot to his car.

CHAPTER 7

1977, Germany

MORE OFTEN, IN fact, most nights, I ended up sleeping on the couch. With Mama watching over me. When nightmares woke me, I looked for her, craving calm, but I couldn't hear her comforting whisper. I became sullen and gloomy. Opa tried all the tricks to cheer me up.

"Let's go to the market for Würstchen," he'd cajole. "Or maybe we can find a ladybug in the shop?" Even trips to the planetarium had lost their luster. *What's the point? I'll have ladybugs and Würst and visions of the moon. But no Opa.* Lack of sleep and my terror that I'd never hear Mama again held me hostage.

"Let's play the money game," Opa replied.

◆◆◆

Normally, I'd jump at the chance to play the money game. Opa would hide twenty deutsche marks in the apartment, and I'd set out to find it. I'd peek into the umbrella stand at the front door. There was an umbrella for each of us—mine had ladybugs and daisies—but no money.

"*Kalt, kalt, sehr kalt!*" Cold. Very cold. I was looking in the wrong place. I moved toward the small bathroom—the one used for number two only—and held my nose as I checked behind the waste basket. The closer I got to the hidden treasure, the more excited he'd become. *Warmer, warmer* until he was practically jumping up and down. "*Heiss, heiss, heiss.*" And then he would take me to spend my money on something special—usually stationery or pens from the bookstore at the train station.

◆ ◆ ◆

"*Kalt, kalt,*" Opa teased. I sighed in exasperation.

"I don't want to play anymore, Opa," I said. But the stricken look on his face convinced me to keep going. For his sake. I walked into Opa's bedroom. Straight to his coveted pencil case. "*Nein, kalt!*" he yelled, bouncing up and down and making his belly jiggle in excitement. I giggled, giving into my connection with my grandfather. Wandering down the long hallway, I paused by the mirror above the armoire to admire my newfound height—I'd grown enough that I could just see the top of my head in the reflection.

"*Es wird heiss,*" Opa said. It's getting hot. As I got closer to the prize, my spirits warmed up too.

The money was not anywhere in the hallway. Not in any flowerpots or tucked under the telephone.

I opened the living room door, and Opa started to hop up and down. "*Warmer, warmer!*" His excitement was contagious, and my heart pounded faster. I walked over to the dining room table. "*Nein, kalter.*" I was perplexed. I knew he wouldn't hide the money in the kitchen. No financial transactions occurred there—it was a superstition, though I didn't know why until I was older. It had been in the kitchen that Opa handed his daughter the airline ticket to America along with a check to get her through her first few months as a college student in Upstate New York. From that moment on, he considered it bad luck to conduct financial business in the sanctuary of the kitchen. I headed toward the couch as Opa's face turned bright red.

"Yes, yes, *heiss, sehr heiss!*" he called. I sat on the couch next to my pillow, and he cried out, "It's burning!" I turned over the pillow and squealed. There was a crisp, unwrinkled twenty deutsche mark. Lying next to it was a black jewelry box.

"What's this?" I asked, holding up the mysterious box. Opa motioned for me to open it. Inside lay a heart-shaped gold locket on a dainty gold chain. I gasped at its beauty, its delicate craftsmanship.

"Open it," he urged. My breath caught in my throat. Inside was a miniature version of my mother's portrait. It was perfect, down to the smallest detail: her curly red hair, her sparkling green eyes, her gentle smile. I held the locket close to my heart, feeling a wave of love and calm. It was the most precious gift I had ever received.

"Now maybe it won't be so scary to go to America. You can carry her with you always," Opa said. He sat on the couch next to me and wrapped his arms around me. He hummed the theme song from *Heidi* and held me as I wept—both from the beauty of his gift and how frightened I was to leave him. I tucked the deutsche marks in my wallet.

"Opa, I'll spend it when we come back to visit you." *We could walk to the store to buy a lotto ticket or buy an ice cream at the Schlossgarten.* And with that, I had my mother to carry with me to my new home and the money that promised I'd always come back to my first home.

CHAPTER 8

1990, East Coast, United States

"HEY, GIRLIE." MIKE Donohue still had never called me by my name, but he included me now in casual conversations.

"Join us for study group at Titan's Bar tonight." It wasn't an invitation but a command.

"I thought that was just for serious theology students. You know, seminarians who can actually become priests in the Catholic Church?" I'd also become better at teasing him back and standing up to him on occasion.

"While it is true that the seminarians will have a leg up on you in terms of intellectual rigor, I'm certain that, with some nourishment and beer, you will have a perspective to add that might be informative." I lobbed my pencil eraser at him. "Nice throw, Saskia," he said. "For a girl." Only a few blocks from campus, I walked to Titan's Bar. Once inside, it took my eyes a minute to adjust to the dim light, but then I spotted their table.

"Come on over, girlie." Mike waved me over and greeted me by throwing his arms around my shoulder.

"Watch out, Mike," I teased. "I've got cooties." I made light of his touch, but inside I was glowing. I was becoming a part of this community. There was an empty wooden chair next to Allen. I got the sense that maybe he planned it that way.

"Mind if I take this seat?" I asked. He gestured for me to sit. A man of few words when we weren't in the library. He was wearing his black leather motorcycle gear. He smelled of Drakkar Noir. *Forbidden things shouldn't smell so good.* I grinned. *Maybe I can catch a ride home on the back of his bike. Arms wrapped around him. Platonic, of course, the passenger on a bike* has *to put their arms around the driver.*

"What happens at these study sessions?" I asked. The guys laughed. Judging by the number of beer bottles on the table, they'd be a lot more relaxed than they usually were in class.

"Define study?" Henry said and pointed toward the empty beer bottles and peanut shells strewn on the table. The guys. The most studious and shy seminarian in class, Henry rarely spoke. When he did, it was always something wise and insightful.

"Ah, I see," I said. "A euphemistic study session."

"Here at Titan's, we are students of life," Henry said and nodded vigorously, fueled by beer and his classmates' laughter. "But we don't usually have girls here, so this 'study session' could be interesting," Henry said. Alcohol was the equalizer. In their uninhibited state, the guys loosened up, and the icy reception I sometimes got in class was melting away. Titan's Bar turned a blind eye to things like a legal drinking age, so I drank a Sam Adams and relaxed into the banter. I could feel Allen's knee pressing against mine. Whether because the table was crowded or on purpose, I couldn't really tell. But I hoped it was on purpose. *What the hell? Where was this coming from? And that smile. I'd do a lot to have that smile directed just at me.*

"Saskia, we don't know much about you. We all live together in the Francis House, so we know everything about each other, but what about you?" Allen asked. My heart was pounding and my hands shaking. *What am I, sixteen?* It was one thing to meet for studying. It was another to have him focus attention on me in front of his peers. *Relax! He's asking to be polite. This doesn't mean anything. He wants them to think he doesn't know me at all.* His question sparked an evening of grilling, and I poured my heart out, savoring the undivided attention of these young men embarking on a life of celibacy in service of God. Being the object of their fascination was intoxicating, tantalizing.

"Why are you studying theology?" Allen asked as though he didn't know. I repeated the story I'd shared with him.

"Well, I spent my life chasing God, and now I've found Her." I smiled, knowing the reference to the feminine would get a rise out of Mike.

"Girlie, we let you come tonight. Don't push your luck." As the questions grew more intimate and a second beer found its way into my hand, a few secrets tumbled out. Safety seemed like an afterthought, if I thought about it at all. The intoxication from the combination of attention and alcohol left me feeling invincible and impervious to vulnerability.

I'm not sure when Father Hamilton arrived. I hadn't been paying attention to who was coming and going. But something in the air had shifted. The men didn't stop asking questions or temper their comments, but they were obviously performing for him.

"So, Saskia," said Tim, one of the older seminarians. He'd had a previous career and a fiancé before he found his calling. "How old were you when you had your first kiss?"

Allen's hand brushed my leg. Emboldened, I responded, "Boy or girl?" And just like that, he drew his hand away.

A chorus of "do tell" rang out, so I did. At that point, I didn't really care if Allen approved or not; the cheering on of his peers propelled me forward.

"The first girl I kissed was Mindy Peterman in fourth grade. The first boy I kissed was Luke Davis, also in fourth grade. We were all in the same class." I hadn't thought about Mindy in a long time. I still felt a twinge of regret that I hadn't tried harder to figure out where she went. "Mindy came home with me from school one day. My nanny, Helga, refused to give her milk and cookies. Helga always gave my friends milk and cookies. But she refused because I called her my girlfriend." It felt good to speak these words out loud. The guys made me feel safe. Seminarians, yes, but human beings too, I was beginning to recognize.

"Was that the only girl you kissed?" Tim teased.

I could have denied it. Could have insisted that it was a silly fourth-grade crush. Maybe things would have turned out differently if I'd stayed in the closet that night. But the feeling in my gut that Mama was telling me to stay true to myself was undeniable.

"No. It wasn't. There have been a few. I'm bisexual." The words were out, and there was no taking them back.

"What does that mean, exactly?" Allen asked. His tone had changed. More combative.

"It means that I am emotionally, spiritually, and physically attracted to both men and women," I explained.

"So, doesn't that just mean you're on your way to being a lesbian?" Mike challenged.

"You're going to spew stereotypes at me, Mike?" I was feeling feisty—and socially lubricated. "Are you a pedophile?" I asked. The words were out of my mouth before I could take them back. No longer in control of any decorum. I quickly moved away from the taboo topic. "I'm sure you think I'm greedy and promiscuous too?" I enjoyed watching Mike turn red and squirm. "Would you like me to pick a side?" I demanded. "Because I fall in love based on hearts, not parts. A lack of the latter would exclude you." The others were cheering me on. They may all kowtow to Mike, but they were delighted that someone was taking him on. Except Allen. Sullen and quiet, he ordered a fourth beer.

"Okay, truce," Mike capitulated. "Let's debate something relevant."

"Like whether you're an asshole or not?" This time, I wouldn't let him have the last word.

There was actually no studying at the study session. Father Hamilton encouraged the banter, and after his third beer, he joined in.

"Fair game, Donohue," Father Hamilton said. "When did you kiss your first boy?" I thought Mike was going to jump up and punch the priest.

"Calm down, young man," Father Hamilton said. "Assuming you're gay because you're becoming a priest is as dangerous as making assumptions about Saskia's orientation." Turns out, Father Hamilton got the last word on the topic.

"Thanks, Father," I said, surprised by the unlikely ally. Shortly before last call, Allen got up to use the bathroom. He stumbled a bit, and as he walked past me, his hand brushed my sweater. Father Hamilton slipped into Allen's seat and whispered in my ear, "You know that he likes you. You should give it a shot." My face must have shown my shock. "His faith will be tested in one way or another. If he's meant to be a priest, he'll be a priest. I'm just not entirely sure he knows what he really wants. What do you have to lose?" Even though every alarm bell in my body was going off, I was drunk and not entirely in control of my actions. And now I had permission to act on my feelings. I pressed my hands against the locket. *Not now, Mama.* I ignored the sense of dread bubbling just below the surface.

CHAPTER 9

March 1977, Germany

On a cold, rainy morning shortly after my seventh birthday, I walked into Magdalena's for what turned out to be the last time. The geraniums seemed to droop, as though absorbing my sadness. Opa was tending to a few chores before he turned the store over to Oma at the train for the day. He was driving us to the airport. Though he had spoken very few words to Papa, he couldn't bear not seeing his granddaughter off on her grand, new adventure. Both men had tried their best to convince me that America would be wonderful, but I was practically inconsolable.

I peppered them with a barrage of questions.

"Where will I go to school since I don't know very much English?" Papa assured me I knew more English than I thought, and that because I was so young, I'd pick up my new language in no time.

"Who will watch me when Papa is at work?" Of course, there was an answer for that.

"Helga," he replied. The German woman who owned the house we'd rent in the States.

"What if I don't like the food?"

"Well, you like bacon, right?" he asked. I had tried American-style bacon once, and I never forgot it. "They eat bacon almost every morning for breakfast," Papa reassured me.

"But I don't like peanut butter, and I heard that American kids eat peanut butter instead of Nutella." Papa promised he would take Nutella with us.

"But I also suspect we'll be able to find it in America," he said.

"What if the other kids don't like me?"

Opa handled this one. "Saskia, there will always be people who don't like you. For many reasons or no reason at all. And that might hurt your feelings. But there will be many more people, like your papa and me and all your omas and Frau Lehman and Frau Sturm, who will like you very much."

And the question that weighed most heavily on my mind. I had the same nightmare repeatedly. I'd wake in the middle of the night, sweat soaking my bedsheets and the salt of my tears staining my cheeks. Opa and Papa both tried to get me to talk about the nightmare, but I didn't dare say it out loud. I didn't want to encourage the possibility that it would come true.

But the night before we left, the night before the worst day of my life, I finally confessed during Magic Circle. I went into the kitchen and pulled the Nutella from the shelf. I got three spoons from the drawer. Then I asked Opa to make the coffee and Papa to meet us around the kitchen table.

"Ah," Opa said, "this must be very important." I nodded.

"More important than anything I've told you in Magic Circle before," I said solemnly.

We each sat on our stools, scooped a spoonful of Nutella, and dipped it into the coffee Opa had poured into the green ceramic mugs with owls on them. Opa drummed his fingers on the table, signaling the start of the circle.

"What is so important, Saskia?" Papa asked. I took a deep breath, still worried that if I said it out loud, I would risk it becoming true. But my father and grandfather needed to know just how seriously they were interfering with my life.

"I'm afraid that when we move to America, I won't be able to hear Mama anymore." My quiet tears turned into sobs, and Opa took me into his arms and rocked me as he had when I was younger. His own tears mingled with mine. He rocked me until I fell asleep.

The mood was somber.

"Opa, can I sweep the shop once more before we leave?" I asked. He nodded and silently handed me the broom. Even though Opa and I had looked at the moon together the night before and he reminded me that we'd always be looking at the same moon, we knew that nothing would be the same.

"You can come visit us in America, can't you, Opa?" I asked. But Opa was adamant that he'd never get on a plane.

"America stole your mother from me, and now it's stealing you. I want nothing to do with that place," he said.

"But how will I see you, Opa?" Tears welled in my eyes. He brushed his hand against my cheek.

"No tears, Saskia. You'll come back and visit me during your papa's summer breaks. We'll have grand adventures and search for Orion together," he said.

The night before, Opa had turned the telescope to the constellations and pointed me to his favorite: Orion.

"You see his long sword in the sky?" Opa asked. I could clearly see the night hunter's sword.

"If you look to the brightest star, you'll find his dog, Sirius." Opa was choking up but tried to regain his composure. I took his hand.

"Opa, I see Orion and Sirius." His hand tightened around mine.

"Then not only will we be looking at the same moon, but we can always look to the sky for Orion and Sirius." I wrapped my arms around him.

"I don't want to go to America, Opa," I said. "I want to stay here so we can look through the telescope together."

Opa sighed. "If wishes were horses, Saskia." I didn't know what that meant, but I could feel his sadness. It weighed as heavy in my hand as it weighed in my heart.

"The sweeping is all done, Opa." I placed the broom and dustpan in their proper spot at the back of the shop.

"Everything has been watered and put away?" he asked. I nodded.

"Well then, you should pick out your treat from the toy box," he said. But I didn't want more ladybugs. I wanted time to stand still, for Papa to come to his senses and let us stay.

"No thanks, Opa. I don't need a ladybug. They haven't brought me much luck lately." A lump formed in my throat, but I wanted to stay brave. We'd already shed so many tears, I felt like I needed to be watered again before I wilted.

"Well then, there's just one last thing to do." Opa walked to the back of the shop where the pots with just the soil in them were kept. He leaned over the pot and whispered three daffodils into bloom.

"For your broken heart," he said. I picked the daffodils and carried them with me as far as the gate at Frankfurt Airport. Fearing they'd be confiscated, I placed them in my book, a hardback copy of *Heidi*.

"Opa, I will miss you so much." I threw my arms around him and didn't let go until Oma at the train came and pried me away. My surrogate grandmothers watched as Papa and I got in the back seat of Opa's Volkswagen. Frau Sturm presented me with a hand-knit lavender blanket. Frau Trunz called out, "Don't forget to eat your vegetables."

Even Frau Lehman said her goodbyes. "Don't forget your manners, young lady." If I'd blinked, I might have missed her wiping away her tears.

Airports will always be the saddest places for me, sadder even than hospitals. I'd only known people to get better in hospitals, even though I knew that didn't always happen. But I associated airports and airplanes with Mama's death. And now with a sorrow even deeper than death. Opa wrote me a long letter that night after he got home. We'd been in America for about a week when Papa handed me the carefully typed letter.

> *Dear Saskia,*
>
> *I wish we could have a Magic Circle. Because I need to tell you that after I left you and your papa at the airport, I couldn't drive home. For hours, I drove around, feeling lost. It wasn't until I needed to fill my gas tank that I realized I'd been weeping and driving for most of the day.*
>
> *I am afraid too, Saskia. What you said about your mama? I'm afraid that I won't hear her anymore either. Because I heard her every time you laughed. Come back to me soon, my darling. There will be plenty of chores at Magdalena's and more adventures waiting for you. Until then, remember the moon and Orion. The world feels very*

big, and you feel so far away, but when we look at the same moon, we remember the world is smaller than we know and that our hearts are always close.

Your loving Opa.

CHAPTER 10

Christmas, 1989

THE LUFTHANSA 747 touched down on the runway in Frankfurt with little more than a bump and a slight squeal of brakes—"beautiful, precise German landing," Opa would have noted. My nose pressed against the window, and my tears mingled with the condensation on the glass. This moment was always magical for me. The sky somehow bluer, the grass greener. My heart home.

"Ladies and gentlemen, meine Damen und Herren, welcome to Germany. Willkommen in Deútschland." The passengers applauded, and my stomach turned summersaults. I unfasted my seat belt before the warning light had gone off. The tug was as strong as ever. Was it my mother's legacy? Did her stories live in me and I felt the pull so strongly now that I was home, or was it simply that, in minutes, I would claim my bags, proceed through customs, and greet Opa at the *Tréffpunkt?* Like I'd done every summer since moving to America. I'd made the transatlantic flight at least twenty times by now. This time felt different. I was a college freshman, visiting for Christmas break, preparing for the RCIA into the Catholic Church this Easter—the time of the daffodils. More grown up. I looked forward to drinking wine at the kitchen table with my grandfather. Each time I thought there wouldn't be another new thing to learn about Mama, he'd surprise me. Frankfurt Airport felt like home to me. The directional signs were in English and German. I automatically read them in my original language. Now I spoke both languages fluently—without an accent. And more often than not, I now dreamed in English, but for a few weeks before an anticipated visit, I'd start dreaming in German again.

<hr>

"Saskia, wake up, you're dreaming," Allen said. After my first study session at Titan's Bar, we'd become as inseparable as two people forbidden to each other could be. We still studied in the library fishbowl with seminarians walking by and checking in. But more often now, we walked to the grotto and talked on a bench with the Virgin Mary watching over us. For weeks, she kept us from acting on our now obvious physical attraction. Allen would walk me back to the dorm and give me a hug at the front door. Maybe it was the anticipation of being apart over Christmas break. Maybe I was wondering if things would be the same after I got back. Preparations for Easter and my conversion would intensify. Or maybe it was just inevitable, but the night before I left for Frankfurt, I invited Allen up to my dorm room. Lisa had already left for the break, and the room would be empty. We sat awkwardly on my bed, suddenly insecure and shy. I leaned over and turned on my CD player. Jethro Tull's *Aqualung* album blared.

"He's almost as good a flute player as you are," Allen said.

"God, I'd give anything to be able to play as well as Ian Anderson." Allen put his arm around my shoulder and leaned his face toward mine.

"What else can you do with those lips?" he asked. And then we were kissing. And touching. His hands reached under my shirt. My hands wandered over his body, suddenly too covered with clothing. I started to unbutton his jeans when he pushed my hand away.

"And this is why we study in the library," he said. "I can't, as much as I want to, I just can't." But he promised to stay until I fell asleep. I softly cried myself to sleep. It was just an hour before my alarm was to go off that he woke me from my dream.

"You were talking in German. I have no idea what you were saying. Something about heis/kalt?" The money game. Of course, it was the first thing we'd do when I got to Opa's.

"So, have a good Christmas break, Saskia. And a safe trip." Allen gave me a quick peck on the cheek.

"I'm sorry we won't have a class together next semester," I said. The conversation was awkward and stilted. "Well, I guess since you're my sponsor, we'll still have to spend some time together," I said hopefully. But we knew it wouldn't—or shouldn't—be the same when I got back.

The German sense of personal space is different from Americans. People pressed closer together, and the pungent smell of body odor mixed with the tantalizing scents of fresh bread and wiener schnitzel. The main concourse was lined with restaurants and food carts that immediately made my mouth water. I headed for the Bretzel cart, always my first stop.

"Eine Butter Bretzel und ein Coca-Cola, bitte." I ordered a pretzel with butter and a Coke. Straight from the glass bottle, it always tasted better in Germany. Although, I suspect that had more to do with the fact that I more strongly felt Mama's presence in Deútschland.

I took my time eating the pretzel and then headed to the *Tréffpunkt*—meeting place. Opa always waited for me there. My stomach was doing flips in anticipation of seeing him. I neared our usual meeting spot and looked around. No sign of Opa. He usually stood right at the front of the crowd, carrying a bouquet of daffodils. Instead, I saw a man holding a "Welcome, Saskia Nash" sign, a transport service to pick me up. I guess Opa thought I was more grown up now. I quickly forgot my disappointment when we took the exit out of the airport and onto the Autobahn. In forty minutes, I'd be home. I kept my face plastered to the window. The other cars rushed past. The speed on the Autobahn never failed to surprise me. I noticed the slope-roofed houses with shingled windows. Further up on the hills, they were snow-covered. The trees were bare, and smoke columns harkened families around a cozy fire. I missed the bright green of my summer homecomings. The bright yellow fields of rapeseed flowers. Still, the winter landscape had its own charm. As the miles flew by, my stomach clenched, and butterflies swirled. When we passed the Mann Mobilia building covered with red dots, I started to fidget. Home in less than twenty minutes.

I walked into the apartment building, at once so familiar and so foreign. Opa had sold Magdalena's, and in its place was a residential carpet store. The stairwell no longer smelled of flowers and coffee but like carpet installation and cleaner. I drew a deep breath and walked the five flights to Opa's apartment. I knocked on the door. I could hear a television behind the door, and Opa's voice yelled, "*Ein moment, Saskia. Ich komme.*" He opened the door, and my heart sank. His cardigan hung on his thin body. His face was pale and wrinkled. *When did my grandfather become old?*

His handshake was still vigorous, and the kiss on each cheek was as tender as always. A strange formality to the German reunion. No big hugs and big shows of emotion. I'd become American in that way and longed for him to wrap his arms around me and not let go. Instead, I returned his shake and kissed him on each cheek.

"Let me take your suitcase to your room," Opa said. I let him. I didn't want to hurt his pride. But it was hard to watch how much he struggled with the effort. I followed him into the room and looked around. The same bookshelves with my favorites still lined up on the bottom. The foldout couch that used to be underneath the portrait of Mama was now neatly tucked away.

"You just have to open it up. The bedding is already on there," Opa said.

"Did Frau Lehman do that for you?" I asked. Because my grandfather wouldn't have done it himself.

"Her daughter, Emma. Frau Lehman is in a nursing home now. Her daughter lives next door." More changes.

"I've got a snack waiting for you in the kitchen," Opa said. I started to walk toward the hallway.

"*Kalt! Sehr kalt.*" Opa grinned. The money game. As I approached my stool in the kitchen, he started jumping up and down. "Heiss!" I found 200 euros tucked in my coffee mug.

"Nutella and coffee coming up," he said.

We spent most of my break sitting in that kitchen. No formal magic circles, but each moment was magical. Christmas came and went without any fuss. We put up a tree on Christmas Eve and exchanged gifts after a traditional meal of herring salad, store-bought from Aldi. The night before my return to the States, we got drunk on red wine. I remembered the times I would sneak outside the kitchen and listen to Papa and Opa talk or argue, with smoke wafting out of the kitchen and empty wine bottles on the table. It was strange to be an adult in the place where I'd been such a carefree child. Opa still smoked, and we'd only gone through a bottle of wine. But it was enough social lubrication for some secrets to spill out.

"Opa, I'm bisexual." My hands shook uncontrollably, and I wanted to grab a cigarette from him even though I'd never smoked.

"Are you in love with someone?" he asked. No raised eyebrows, no shocked look. No judgment, just curiosity.

"I am. It's a long story. When I told him I was bisexual, things changed." I poured my heart out. Opa sat and listened and occasionally nodded. I told him all about Allen, that he was in the seminary. That when he'd found out I'd had a girlfriend before—and that it had not been strictly platonic—he said he'd never be able to consider marrying someone who sinned in such a way.

"I don't think he'd consider marrying me anyway. I think he's determined to be a priest. But in the meantime, I'm in way over my head, and I'm not sure I'd be able to say no to him if . . . um . . . things got carried away." Although it was a little weird to be talking about such personal things with my grandfather, it felt good to get it all out. And to be loved. No matter what. Opa took a long drag of his cigarette.

"You deserve more, Saskia." He stubbed out the cigarette in his ashtray and took a sip of his wine. "A man who cannot accept you for who you are is no man for you. And a man who is hedging his bets between God and you is also no man for you. All I've ever wanted for you was your happiness. Whether that happiness comes from being with a man, a woman, or alone, it is only happiness that I wish for you." The wine had reddened his cheeks, and his eyes were leaky.

"I chose to be alone, you know," he said. "Not that I didn't have romances here and there, but after your grandmother, I didn't need anything more. I had a love that was strong, a daughter I adored, and now a granddaughter who is the Sirius to my Orion." I wept. It was the first time he really talked about my grandmother, and I wanted to know more.

"Tell me about her, Opa. About my grandmother. I don't even know her name," I said.

"Her name was Judith. She was smart, funny, stubborn, and opinionated," he said. "I saw my wife in your mother every day. And some days, it was just so painful." His voice trailed off. "I think that is why I was so angry when Petra left for America. I felt abandoned all over again."

Abandoned? "What do you mean by abandoned, Opa?"

He sighed. "Your grandmother loved me, but she was not *in* love with me," he said. "She was in love with Magdalena.

"She left you for another woman?" I asked. He shook his head.

"She left me emotionally for Magdalena." His answer hung in the air. "We still lived together, still lived as husband and wife, with all that means." He blushed. "After all, we had your mother. But her heart belonged to Magdalena." *The flower shop? Is my grandmother bisexual? I'm not a freak?*

"Your oma and Magdalena owned the flower shop. I inherited it when they died." Just as suddenly as I had a bisexual grandmother, I had a dead one.

"They were on a trip to Interlaken—the same cabin where we used to go, where you left your penis." He laughed. "God, you embarrassed me that day on the strassenbahn."

I giggled. "I can only imagine how embarrassing that must have been for you," I said, recalling my very loud insistence on the very public tram that I was most definitely a boy and must have left my penis in Switzerland.

"But what happened to Oma? Would she have wanted me to call her that?"

He lit another cigarette. It was a half-pack night, something he didn't do often anymore, but when secrets spill, the rules could be broken.

"She would have loved it. She doted on Petra. She and Magdalena both did. We had an unusual arrangement. We each had our own bedroom. Your bedroom used to be Magdalena's. I guess we were true bohemians," he mused.

"Petra was with me when they went on that trip to Switzerland. Sometimes they would take her, but this time, Petra was with me." He started to cry. "Sometimes I come close to believing in a god because at least he spared me Petra." I leaned over and put my head on his shoulder.

"They died in a car accident on the trip home. They were only thirty miles from here. Petra was just five."

I looked around the kitchen. My grandmother, her lover, and my grandfather had sat at this very table. So had my mother. With the exception of a new refrigerator and the addition of a dishwasher, this was the same kitchen where they'd made all their important decisions.

"I'm happy your grandmother was happy. She gave me an interesting and exciting life. A friendship with Magdalena that I treasured. A shop that I loved. And my precious daughter who gave me the best gift I've ever known," he said, "you, my darling Saskia. Who deserves to be happy. Don't let yourself get hurt by this seminarian." My mind was whirling. So much about myself was starting to make sense. *There is nothing wrong with me. I'm like my grandmother.* "Yours won't always be an easy life, Saskia. But make it one that is, in balance, always more happy than sad."

The car service rang the apartment bell, and Opa told the driver over the intercom that I was on my way down. I carried my own suitcase. Opa continued to look frail, and this time, he didn't insist on carrying my luggage. Opa shook my hand and kissed me on each cheek. *This stoic, formal interaction is bullshit!* I threw my arms around him. He relaxed into my embrace. Our first and last real hug.

CHAPTER 11

1977, East Coast, United States

AND JUST LIKE that, my fairy-tale childhood came to an end. We were in America. On the East Coast. An ocean away from Opa and everything I'd known and loved. Papa rented a basement apartment from a relative of Omi at the train station. Frau Helga Stein was a widow, the picture of the proper German housewife. She must have been in her early sixties, but to me, she looked ancient. She always wore a long black skirt with a gray sweater and an apron. Her long straight gray hair was pulled back in a bun so tight that she always wore an expression of surprise on her face. And she was my nanny. She ran our household so Papa could work and spoke with me only in German so I wouldn't forget my roots. It was Frau Stein's mission to undo all the "wishy-washy" nonsense Papa and Opa had taught me.

"Ridiculous," she spat. "The Easter Bunny does not make chicken noodle soup, silly child." And then proceeded to tell me the real meaning of Easter. She would quiz me about all things Germany at unexpected times.

"Saskia, tell me who is the current chancellor of Germany," Frau Stein instructed.

"I don't know," I answered. I didn't care or see how it was relevant.

"Gerald Ford is our president," I answered. We were learning about presidents in school.

"We are not American, child. Mr. Ford is not our president. Helmut Schmidt is our chancellor." Frau Stein's purpose in life was to argue with me.

"But Papa says I am American because he's American. And I'm here now so I should be learning about this country," I insisted. Papa tried to run interference. He cajoled Frau Stein into bending just a little to meet me in the middle.

"You spoil that child, Mr. Nash, and she will be nothing but trouble."

And so, he would implore me, "Saskia, try to be more cooperative." And I would try, and fail, to be more cooperative. Frau Stein didn't like me, and it wouldn't matter if I could recite every chancellor in Germany's history.

"Not good enough," she said when I would struggle to read from the German newspaper she picked up from the Black Forest Deli in town.

"I'm just a kid," I would protest. "And I'm learning to read English."

Papa told Frau Stein that I loved bacon. If I'd been particularly good, occasionally, I would get breakfast for dinner . . . complete with bacon. Bacon was a very rare treat, and even then, Frau Stein would find a way to ruin it.

"I don't like burnt bacon," I said.

"And I don't like children who aren't grateful for what is put in front of them," she retorted. And she would sit across from me at the table, staring, until I ate every single charred bite. We spent a great deal of time across the table from each other in a war of wills. The war of wills continued as time went on. Papa spent more time at the university. He'd occasionally take me in the afternoons when school got out early. But most of the time, it was me and Frau Stein.

As much as I disliked Frau Stein, I loved her baking. She made traditional German cookies all year-round. The *Pfeffernüsse* were my favorites—peppernut gingerbread spice cookies. Sometimes I was allowed to have a friend over. Frau Stein would provide cookies and milk. More often than not, the friends I brought home were boys. Frau Stein encouraged my friendships with these boys and eventually encouraged my crushes.

"Saskia has another crush," she reported to Papa. "This time, it's Luke, a curly-haired blond boy with very nice manners." I adored Luke until he threw up on my art project. And then Mindy Peterman joined our fourth-grade class.

CHAPTER 12

February 19, 1990, East Coast, United States

EVERYTHING WAS GRAY in the winter on the East Coast. The skies, the sooty buildings, the snow leftover from a recent dusting. Even the students were subdued on campus. I'll always remember that day as gray. Like remembering where I was when the Challenger exploded. Ms. Ross's sociology class. I was just a few weeks from my fifteenth birthday, and we were excited when we came to class and saw the television set up. You don't forget moments like that. I was sitting next to Peter Bankston, who was eating a Snickers bar. We weren't supposed to eat in class, but Ms. Ross was cool, and she loved me and Peter, her top students.

"Want a bite?" Peter offered. I took that bite, and the world exploded before my eyes. I never had another Snickers bar. I'll always associate the shuttle explosion with Peter Bankston and Snickers.

Peter lives in Philadelphia now with his wife and the children they adopted from China. I wonder if he ever eats Snickers bars.

—•••—

I'll always associate February 19, 1990, with Allen and Skittles. And gray. Of course, I didn't heed Opa's warning about Allen. As soon as I got back to campus, we picked up where we left off. By now, Allen didn't bother with the pretense that he shouldn't come up to my room. He just did. Sometimes Lisa was there, and though she was suspicious, she didn't want to consider that someone called to be a priest would do anything against his vows. More often than not, Lisa was out—studying or at her off-campus job at Perkins.

On that day, we were listening to the Grateful Dead and eating Skittles. We were supposed to be reading Thomas Merton's *Seven Storey Mountain* for our Christian Formation class. Instead, we were goofing around, tossing Skittles at each other, and trying to catch them in our mouths.

The knock on the door startled me. Papa's knock. He tried not to interfere in my college life. We came up with the knock in case of an emergency.

"Oh God," I said. "It's my dad. Something's wrong." I got up from the bed and walked to the door. My legs felt like they were encased in cement. The knock on the door repeated. I opened the door and saw my father standing there with tears flowing down his face. Opa. I knew. And sank to the floor. Papa came and sat next to me. I wished I could crawl into his lap and make the nightmare go away.

"He didn't suffer long, Saskia. A massive heart attack. He probably never even knew what hit him." I sobbed until there was nothing left in me. Papa eventually left. Allen sat awkwardly on my bed.

"Do you want any more Skittles?" he asked. My sobs had subsided into occasional hiccups of tears.

"I want to wake up from this nightmare," I said. "I want Opa to be alive. I want this all to be one terrible dream that I can put out of my mind." But life doesn't work that way. I touched the locket around my neck. But I couldn't feel anything.

"Please just hold me now," I begged. And he did. Allen grabbed my hand and pulled me up from off the floor and lay down beside me on the bed. And then he was kissing my lips and stroking my body.

"Please don't stop," I said. This feeling of guilt and fear and desire jumbled up in me was infinitely better than the unbearable sadness. And he didn't stop. He didn't stop until it was too late. Soon, we were both sobbing again. My tears for Opa and endings. His tears in frustration for having given in to his desires.

"This can't happen again," Allen said. "And no one can know," he added.

"Just go," I said. "It won't happen again. It didn't really happen now. We were both out of our minds." He walked out the door, leaving a half-empty bag of Skittles behind. I picked them up, flung them across the room, and watched them scatter. Then I crawled to pick up each one and stuff them in my mouth. To dull the pain. I stuffed them in my mouth until I couldn't hold anymore. The rush of sugar flooded my body with adrenaline and energy. And then I swallowed them in one chewed-up mass. The agony as they scraped against my esophagus momentarily let me forget about Allen and the ache between my legs. And the Opa-sized gash in my heart.

CHAPTER 13

Late 1970s, East Coast, United States

WOMEN ARE THE secret keepers. The cost for our silence is heavy. For our world. For the boys who learn to mimic their fathers' behaviors and for us, the little girls who grow into young ladies and then women who lose their voice and gain anorexia or depression or anxiety or phobias. I lost my voice when I brought Mindy Peterman home. Helga refused her milk and cookies. I learned to be silent. And I gained an addiction to self-destruction and collecting boys. Papa once said that if he invited all my boyfriends to a cookout, he'd have to rent out an entire football stadium. *And you didn't even know about the girls I desired, Papa.*

I'm a secret keeper.

But in fourth grade, I hadn't yet learned to be silent about liking girls. I'd had boyfriends. Crushes that Helga encouraged. "Isn't that sweet, Mr. Nash?" Papa would roll his eyes and say, "Don't encourage her. We'll regret it later." But in fourth grade, I'd already had boys walk me home. Helga would invite them in, give them milk and a cookie, and send them on their way. Luke Miller had been the most recent boy to escort me home. Before Mindy Peterman transferred into our classroom, Luke had been the most recent boy to get milk and cookies. But then he threw up on my arts and crafts project, one I was making to honor my mother and to spite Helga. My love ran cold. I also had boys who were friends. They didn't walk me home. And most of the time, they were more fun to hang out with than the boyfriends. And I definitely knew the difference between boyfriend and boy who was a friend.

When Mrs. Cappalucci introduced Mindy Peterman to the class, my heart skipped a beat. She was the prettiest girl I had ever seen. And I had girls who were friends. But I wanted this freckle-faced redhead with overalls and a bandanna to walk me home and stay for milk and cookies. I wanted her to be my girlfriend. Mrs. C. assigned me to be Mindy's buddy. I showed her where to hang her coat, how to fill out her library card, and which line to get in at lunch. And every day, we'd go to the playground and pretend we were the Mandrell Sisters and sing, "You can eat crackers in my bed any time, *baby*." We planned to make a recording someday. Sometimes we let the other girls sing backup, but everyone knew that we were the main duo.

"Do you want to come to my house after school and have milk and cookies?" I asked Mindy three weeks after she'd transferred to Centennial Elementary. I told her all about my nanny Helga. That she was strict and didn't like me much, but she made the best Pfeffernüsse.

"But she doesn't just make them at Christmas," I explained. "She likes to show off her German heritage, so she makes German Christmas cookies the whole year. So, do you want to come over and try some?" Mindy blushed a little and turned her head away from me.

"I'll have to ask my foster mom, but yeah, I want to." Mindy grabbed my hand. "Does this mean you're my best friend?" Mindy asked.

I grinned at her. "Nope, it means you're my girlfriend." I leaned over and kissed her on the cheek. "Oh, what's a foster mom?" I asked.

Mindy explained that her mom and dad died in a car accident

when she was four. "I didn't have any other relatives, so I have foster parents. They take care of me like they are my parents, but they aren't, really." Mindy's eyes darkened, and she grew quiet. Not having a mother was just one of the many things we had in common.

"It's okay. I don't have a mom either. And my dad is always at work. Frau Helga is like a foster mother, I guess." And with that, our bond grew stronger. Two days later, Mindy got permission from Mrs. Lytle—her foster mom—to walk home with me, as long as I walked her back to the school afterward so she could pick her up. She shook her head when I offered to have Helga drive Mindy home afterward.

"I'll pick Mindy up right here in front of the school," she insisted. On our walk home, I asked Mindy why Mrs. Lytle didn't want us to drive her all the way home.

"Mind your own business," Mindy snapped. It was the only time she'd ever shown any irritation. I never learned the reason. Except for Mindy's outburst, the walk home that day was perfect. We held hands and laughed and sang. We moved on from the Mandrells to Billy Joel and were perfecting our rendition of "Piano Man." "Sing us a song, we're the piano *man*," we cried in unison. Harmony was not really our strength, but enthusiasm, we had in spades. I wanted to hurry home to introduce Mindy to Helga and Papa, and I wanted to linger so the walk would never end. I think it is the last time I felt pure joy and excitement and anticipation. The last few moments of thinking the world was kind and fair and accepting.

"Helga, Papa, we're home!" Helga sat at the kitchen table in her bathrobe with curlers in her long blond hair. Her eyes were bloodshot and her hands shaking. This was highly unusual. I rarely saw Helga in anything but her starched black skirt, a white blouse, and a gray cardigan sweater. And her hair was always pulled back in a severe bun that pulled her eyebrows toward her hairline.

"What's wrong," I asked. "Where's Papa?"

"None of your concern," she hissed. "And your father is working.

Where did you think he was?" Helga had always been unaffectionate and cold, but her tone was downright nasty.

It was then she glanced over and noticed that I had company.

"Who's this?" she asked.

"Helga, I'd like to introduce you to my girlfriend, Mindy Peterman." Helga's first task when we moved in had been to teach me the manners she believed Opa and Papa had neglected to teach me.

"You introduce me as Frau Stein, young lady," she scolded. "And girls don't have girlfriends, Saskia," she said. Mindy held out her hand to shake Helga's. The gesture was ignored. "You meant that Mindy is a girl who is your friend," Helga clarified. "Your English is very good, but you must be precise so people won't misunderstand."

Defiant, I responded, "No, she's my girlfriend." Mindy blushed and put down her hand, and her cheeks reddened with embarrassment. I grabbed Mindy's hand and kissed her on the cheek. "Now let's have milk and cookies," I demanded. I didn't understand why Helga was so mad that I insisted Mindy was my girlfriend. But I could feel her rage, and I felt shame.

Helga stood up and towered over me. *"Not in this house!"* Her robe had started to slip, and she quickly covered herself, then aimed her right pointer finger at the door. "Out, now!"

The walk back to school was excruciating. I held Mindy's hand and told her she was still my girlfriend, but we'd have to keep it a secret from the grown-ups. She didn't say a word. Mrs. Lytle picked Mindy up in front of the school, and Mindy slipped into the back of the baby-blue VW Beetle before I could say anything else.

"Thank you for having Mindy over," Mrs. Lytle said with a wave. I never saw Mindy again. Mrs. C tried to console me.

"Foster kids often move around a lot. We don't know where Mindy went. There was no forwarding address, just a note that she was switching schools." I was inconsolable. I blamed myself. And Helga.

Women are the secret keepers. And so, I kept my secret—the

truth of who I was—and started collecting boys like trophies. It was easy for Helga to think that Mindy—and everything that episode had implied—was just a phase. I don't know if she ever said anything to Papa. But it was a secret that I knew I could never tell—not even in Magic Circle.

I never brought home another girl. One boy after the other would come home for milk and cookies, then, as we grew older, Coca-Cola and potato chips. Helga and I settled into a détente. I got good grades throughout middle and high school. I played the flute in the marching band and orchestra. I spoke German better than my German teachers, and I picked up French, smiling when I remembered learning to conjugate French verbs with Opa during Magic Circle.

I applied to colleges but never really intended to go anywhere other than where Papa taught. A professor's salary wasn't enough to afford a private college somewhere else. And the tuition waiver I received as his daughter meant no student loans for me. It was a no-brainer.

Papa took an apartment near campus with an extra bedroom for me. Frau Stein took on other tenants, another German family new to the States. I felt sorry for the young boy. But maybe he'd like burnt bacon. I knew he would like her cookies and milk.

That summer before my freshman year, I fell in love with my manager at Kentucky Fried Chicken. Lucy and I were inseparable. But she was a couple years older and had a boyfriend, and I didn't need my heart broken again. "We can still see each other. It's not as though you're going to college a million miles away," Lucy said.

"My heart can only take so many goodbyes in a lifetime, Lucy,"

I said. "And in the end, you will choose Timothy over me, and I'll fall in love with a man because it's just easier that way." Lucy married Tim. They had two children and divorced three years later. I compartmentalized my feelings. Lucy went into the segment with Mindy Peterman that I kept locked up and unexamined. It was just easier that way.

CHAPTER 14

Holy Thursday, April 12, 1990

CHOIR REHEARSALS FOR Holy Week kept my attention focused on anything but the pregnancy. And by the time we came to Holy Thursday, I had neatly compartmentalized my feelings. I was becoming an expert in that. Papa and I didn't return to Germany again after the funeral. There was no reason to. We had picked out a few things from the apartment—I wanted Opa's stamp collection, his writing utensils, and the cardigan he was wearing when he died. The buttons were mismatched, and that's how I kept them. The cardigan held a faint scent of cigarettes and wine and daffodils. When I wore it, I could go back to that kitchen, sit on that stool, and taste Nutella dipped in coffee. My happy place. I lived in that cardigan.

Holy Week is the Boston Marathon of the Catholic liturgical calendar. My first Holy Thursday. By the next Thursday, I'd be a woman who aborted her child. But tonight, in a ritual celebrating Jesus as a humble servant of his people, the sanctuary was filled with barefooted students and faculty ready to participate in an act so intimate, so personal, it shook me to the core. Wooden bowls were placed around the sanctuary—full of warm water that Father Hamilton had blessed.

"When he washed their feet and put on his outer garments again, he went back to the table. 'Do you understand,' he said, 'what I have done to you? You call me Master and Lord, and rightly: so I am. If I then, the Lord and Master, have washed your feet, you must wash each other's feet.'" Father Hamilton's deep bass voice carried through the room. As he finished reading the gospel, he turned toward his acolyte—Allen, of course. Father Hamilton picked up a bowl of water. A white towel was draped around his right arm. He got down on his knees before Allen, who stepped into the bowl. Father Hamilton placed his hands on Allen's feet and washed them as Jesus had washed his disciples' feet. I stifled the urge to giggle out loud. *Can you smell his disgusting feet? And see the athlete's foot? That is not in the spirit of Jesus.*

When he was through, Allen stepped out of the bowl, and Father Hamilton toweled off his feet. With that gesture, he turned toward the congregation and began instructions for washing each other's feet. I was relieved that I was playing the flute in the choir. We didn't have to participate in the ritual. The thought of accepting such a kindness on behalf of Jesus made me feel ashamed.

As it was, the music broke my heart. I started to play the descant to the "Foot Washing Song," but I couldn't continue.

"I, who made the moon and stars, am here to wash your feet." The choir sounded angelic. Our music director caught my eye and gave me a quizzical look. Carl wasn't one to judge or get angry. I knew he'd forgive my performance. I could see in his eyes, though, he knew it wasn't because of performance anxiety.

"What happened, Saskia?" he asked me after the service. "Are you okay?" The compassion in his gentle eyes brought me to my knees.

"It must be the nerves of preparing to be initiated into the church," I lied. That seemed to be my life these days. Lying to myself, to Papa, to everyone around me. And as I was about to become fully baptized into the Catholic Church in just two nights, the biggest lie of all—that I was a faithful servant of the Catholic faith. I longed to hear my mother's voice and held the locket in my hand in hopes I'd hear her. But either she wasn't whispering, or I wasn't listening to her voice tell me I had another choice.

<hr />

I walked a burdened walk back to the dorm. I considered stopping on the second floor and avoiding confession. But my feet carried me to the third floor, where Father Hamilton had his dorm room. It didn't occur to me to wonder why he was hearing my confession in his room. Our sanctuary didn't have confessionals, so face-to-face confessions were fairly common, or so I thought. Having a first confession was something I was supposed to do before the Easter Vigil anyway, so one way or another, I was going to have to go through with it. I knocked softly on the door, hoping he wouldn't hear me and I could sneak away.

"Come in, Saskia, the door's open," he said.

So much for my escape. I had never been in Father Hamilton's room before. It looked remarkably like a regular dorm room. Small bed, gray walls, mini refrigerator, and a plain wooden desk. But the resemblance ended there. The walls were covered with icons. I recognized St. Rose of Lima and The Good Shepherd. Mary of Medjugorje. There was a coffee table in the middle of the room with a single candle in the middle and a leather copy of *The New Jerusalem Bible*. And there was a small crimson couch—more like a love seat—behind the coffee table. Above the couch was Jesus, with outstretched hands, on the cross. Nail marks visible. Tears carved into the wooden cheeks.

"It's beautiful, isn't it?" Father Hamilton saw me staring at the crucifix. "Go ahead and sit down on the couch," he invited.

"I don't know how to do this," I said. He sat down next to me and put his hand on my knee.

"Just follow my lead," he instructed. "I'll start with a scripture reading. Isaiah 43:1, which demonstrates that not only does God love you, but He knows you by name." The same verse he mentioned the first time I met him. Weird. He reached for the Bible. I never noticed how feminine his hands looked. Fingernails too long, the palms hairless and covered in freckles.

"And God knows your sin before you commit it," Father Hamilton said. "And my own, for that matter." And with that, he started to read from Isaiah. The Bible was just a prop. He had the text memorized.

"Turn to face me, dear Saskia," he said and began to recite. In front of me was my confessor. Above me, Jesus on the cross. And those things—a priest and my savior—should have made me feel safe. Instead, I felt as though my locket was strangling me.

"Run," I heard Mama whisper. "You don't have to do this." But I was paralyzed.

I cringed when Father Hamilton placed his hands on my face. I could smell the scotch on his breath, a smell that, to this day, makes me shiver in disgust.

"And now, thus says Yahweh, he who created you, Jacob, who formed you, Israel. Do not be afraid, for I have redeemed you," he read. "Do you hear that, Saskia? He redeems you." His hands stroked my cheeks. "I have called you by your name, Saskia. You are mine," he recited as if in a trance. His eyes bore into mine. His hands moved from my face to my shoulders. I stiffened.

"Should you pass through the waters, I shall be with you; or through rivers, they will not swallow you up. Should you walk through fire, you will not suffer, and the flame will not burn you."

With Jesus watching, Father Hamilton placed his hands on my breasts and then lowered them to my lap. He sighed.

"We are all sinners, Saskia, even me. The time isn't right for you to be a mother. And as much as that pains you, you'll thank me someday for making this choice." Tears streamed down my face. But he misunderstood them.

"I wish I could hold you all night long in my arms, darling Saskia. But that would just add sin upon sin." He brought his hands slowly against my breasts again, then abruptly stood up and knelt before me.

"Jesus forgives you, Saskia. God, the father of mercies, through the death and resurrection of his Son, has reconciled the world to himself and sent the Holy Spirit among us for the forgiveness of sins. Through the ministry of the church, may God give you pardon and peace, and I absolve you from your sins in the name of the Father and of the Son and of the Holy Spirit. Amen." I did not echo his amen. Yes, he misunderstood my tears. I was crying for my unborn child, but mainly I was crying because, in just two days, I was going to be baptized and consume the body and blood of a god I no longer believed in.

Maybe the flame wouldn't burn me. But the shame was searing through me. Years later, my nightmares were filled with flames and rushing waters and grotesque crucifixes coming to life and chasing after me. What made them worse was knowing that Allen—Father Tucker, he would be in just a few short years—and his savior—Father Hamilton—slept like babies.

CHAPTER 15

Good Friday, April 13, 1990, Easter Vigil

IT WASN'T LOST on me that Good Friday was on Friday the thirteenth, the day of superstitions and bad omens. Many people believe that Good Friday is called so because it is good that Jesus died to redeem us. But the medieval use of the word means holy. There was nothing good about that day.

Six weeks in, and I should have scheduled my first prenatal doctor's appointment by now. I was still sick most mornings, always fatigued. My breasts were tender and my stomach bloated. No one would be able to look at me and say, "She's pregnant." But I knew. According to the research I'd done in the library—a way of torturing myself—I knew the fetus was about the size of a large sesame seed. If the book had said "speck," or maybe "spot," any word other than seed, I might have been spared additional agony. But that word, "seed." Something that could grow into something else. Except that this seed wouldn't. Good Friday turned into Holy Saturday. What should have been a day of rejoicing—my initiation into the church—was a day of dread. We had choir rehearsal in the morning, followed by a luncheon for the musicians. Then another rehearsal for the initiates in the afternoon.

The Mass went by in a blur. I didn't hear a word of Father

Hamilton's homily. I have very little recollection of my baptism or taking first communion. It may as well have been a bath and eating a piece of cardboard. The meaning of the sacraments were lost on me now. I plastered a smile on my face. I saw Papa in the congregation. A first for him. As an atheist, he didn't participate in religious ceremonies but wanted to be there to support me. *I'm so sorry, Papa. I wish I could do things all over again.*

The choir sang the "Litany of Saints" and "Veni Sancte Spiritus." The chorus of saint names, followed by the congregational response, "pray for us," seemed to last an eternity. Allen was expecting me to take Teresa as my confirmation name. But I had changed my mind.

The deacon approached me with the chrism. Allen, as my sponsor, stood behind me with his hand on my shoulder.

"What name does the candidate choose as their own?" the deacon droned. I was the sixth confirmand, and he was going through the motions. I hesitated for a moment and then said, "I take the name Perpetua," I proclaimed. Allen's hand grabbed my shoulder tighter. I could feel the anger coursing through him.

"Saskia Perpetua Nash, I seal you with the gift of the Holy Spirit." The deacon traced the sign of the cross with the chrism on my forehead. I wore a wide smile. I could feel Papa's eyes on me. "I'm so happy for you," he mouthed. Let them think the wide smile was a smile of joy. But the smile was for Allen. He knew the lives of the saints backward and forward. He would understand the choice I'd chosen, Saint Perpetua. Patroness of mothers, expectant mothers, ranchers. And butchers.

⊰ · ⊱

I woke up on Easter morning in a cold sweat. I had tossed and turned most of the night. I couldn't get comfortable, and waves of nausea rushed over me throughout the night. I'd sleep for a few minutes and then wake up aching all over. I tried to vomit a few times, but the nausea was spiritual. I'd finally fallen fast asleep when I began to dream. I was in a wide field of wilted daffodils. They smelled of death and rot, and my eyes were blinded by their bright yellow. I kept hearing a voice. "Mama, help me." Over and over again. In the distance, I saw him. His hands were reaching for me, outstretched. He had blue eyes and curly blond hair. An angel's face. I reached my arms out toward him, but there was a large gorge in between us—like the gorge at *Hirschsprung*. I knew the little boy was looking for the Easter Bunny. "Come help me, Mama!" he yelled. But I just stood there. In the field of wilted daffodils. "Just jump," he screamed. "We need to find the Easter Bunny. We lost the chicken noodle soup recipe. We need to find it before Easter." But I just stood there, frozen to that spot. The distant sound of my son echoed in my head, and the smell of rotting daffodils assaulted my nostrils. And I just stood there.

CHAPTER 16

Monday, April 16, 1990

THE DRIVE FROM campus to the local Planned Parenthood seemed excruciatingly long, even though it was just a few miles. Father Hamilton barely spoke a word to me. His silence and his hand on my knee for the duration of the ride spoke volumes. I wanted to rip his hand off my knee and crush it in my fist. I wanted him to feel an unending physical pain to match my psychic pain. Allen tried to speak to me after confirmation, but I turned him away. There were no words left to say to him.

As we approached the nondescript, small brick building, Father Hamilton slowed down and pulled into a spot a few houses away from our destination. He turned to face me.

"Saskia, I know this is difficult for you," he said. I couldn't look him in the eye. He reached out to touch my shoulder, and I brushed him away. I loathed his touch. He continued, "Allen is our top seminary student, and he has a promising career as a priest ahead of him. Who knows, maybe even bishop or cardinal." I nodded.

"We've had this conversation, Father," I said. "I know what's expected of me."

And a baby wouldn't fit into those plans. And giving it away for adoption would leave too many possibilities of blowing his cover down the road. And we should be punished for the sin of having fallen in love. *I get it, Father Hamilton. We fucked up. But doesn't the church consider what I'm doing today EVIL?* I just nodded at Father Hamilton. I felt the cash in my pocket weigh me down like a noose around my neck. Enough for the procedure, and he had slipped in more than enough to keep me silent. He handed me a business card. "Once you're finished, call a taxi and give them this address. Lester will take care of you during spring break, and you'll finish out the semester doing your community service immersion. I assume you've let Lisa know that you won't be on campus for several weeks." I nodded. Lisa had been so excited for me. She wouldn't be able to do her community service immersion semester until the following year. She was envious of me. Ha! I wouldn't wish this on anyone.

"God, I wish I could do my immersion early. You're so lucky," Lisa said. She had bought the explanation that Pippin House needed immediate volunteers, and I was the only one who expressed any interest in working with the gay men.

"You're so brave to work with those men," she said. "And it will help you get over the miscarriage," Lisa said. She was still the only one on campus besides Allen and Father Hamilton who'd known about the pregnancy. Miscarriage seemed like an easy lie; of course, it had been Father Hamilton's suggestion.

"Allen's being reassigned to another seminary, and you won't see each other again. You'll return to campus at the beginning of next semester, and no one will know anything ever happened," said Father Hamilton. I opened the car door and started to get out.

"Wait," he said. "In time, Saskia, you will forgive me, and you'll forgive Allen. And I pray that you'll forgive the church," he said. "It's important that no one knows, Saskia. It's best for everyone in the end." Except for me. And the seed that might have become something more. I doubted I would ever forgive.

I opened the door and stepped out of the car without saying another word. He'd have my silence. Women have always been silenced. But I would know the truth. Others might see him as a hero or "what-a-waste" and believe him to be a holy man of the cloth. But I knew better.

He was no hero. He was the embodiment of the bogeyman Opa had sworn to protect me from.

The walk from the parking spot to the front doors of Planned Parenthood was the longest walk of my life. My heart ached, the lump in my throat threatened to choke me, and I swore I could feel movement inside me, even though at just six weeks along, it was probably only my imagination.

At the fence to the clinic, a handful of protesters stood with signs or knelt in prayer. I recognized a few students from campus, but I had on sweats and a hoodie, and I kept my head down. The voices echoed around me, but I drowned them out. I didn't need their words to remind me that what I was doing was wrong for me. I was vehemently pro-choice. But also very much aware that this was not my choice. Just before I reached the entrance, I saw three daffodils. The Easter Bells. A sign of hope and beginnings. That somehow things would be okay. *Thank you, Opa. But you don't know what I'm about to do. Maybe those daffodils should be wilted.*

I remember nothing of the procedure. I know the doctor performed a suction abortion using vacuum aspiration to empty my uterus. Clinical. Cold. Medically safe. A procedure that should be legal. I believed in that choice with all my heart. It just had never occurred to me that I'd ever be in a position to choose this option. I don't remember checking in or speaking with a counselor. Or being called to the room where I would lose my baby. In my daydreams, I'd imagined getting up just as the procedure got underway. Leaving the clinic, defiant and relieved. But I don't remember if I even tried to get up and leave. I don't remember seeing the doctor or any of the preparations. Somehow, I must have gotten into the surgical gown.

My first memory was after the procedure. I was dressed again, still lying on the procedure table. There was a television in the room. I noticed that it was unplugged from the wall. I wondered why anyone would want to watch television anyway. I wasn't sure if I was supposed to wait until a nurse came into the room or if I was free to go. My abdomen was cramping, but what I felt more than anything was an empty hollowness. I was groggy and kept closing my eyes.

I opened my eyes and stared at the television screen. A small baby boy floated on the screen, reaching his hand out to me. He wore blue overalls and a train conductor's hat. His tiny feet were bare, and he had the most beautiful, tiny, upturned nose and a laugh that I would treasure in my heart for always.

"Mama," he whispered. "Mama, I found the Easter Bunny."

I sat up and reached toward the television, clutching my locket, and for the first time in so long, I felt my own mother's presence.

"Mama," I implored. "Take care of my Max, wherever you are." And then I cried until there were no more tears. I left the clinic and called a taxi. The driver asked where I was going. I gave him the address to Pippin House. I looked at the card more closely. In Calibri font and rainbow colors, it advertised, *Pippin House: a Halfway House for Men Living with AIDS.*

I giggled. When Father Hamilton told me of the arrangements, I hadn't given it much thought. The irony. They were sending me to a home for people the church considered outcasts. A perfect fit.

CHAPTER 17

April 16, 1990, Pippin House

HE DUMPED HIS pain—messy and sticky and heavy—in my lap, and his rage flew out his mouth, the spittle spotting my glasses. I'd been at Pippin House for a little more than half an hour . . . long enough for a cursory tour of the home, a brief introduction to the "guests," and Ed Smith to decide he didn't like "that new sickly-looking straight White bitch." My pale skin felt unusually pasty, and my hands pressed into my stomach—pushing against the physical cramping. A constant reminder.

"Ed, that's no way to treat the nice new volunteer, sweetie," Lester said in a gentle, soothing tone. The soft voice was unexpected coming from the giant redheaded man in tight black leather pants. Lester rushed over to me to help clean up the heap of creamed corn in my lap and wiped the Ensure from my glasses.

"I'm so sorry," Lester fussed. "He can't help himself. He has HIV-related encephalopathy. He acts out sometimes."

"And don't call me Ed, you asshole," he screamed at Lester. "I am Marlena Merlot."

My mind was a whirlwind. *Encephalopathy? Marlena Merlot?* I felt weak from the surgery—and from the surreal surroundings. Lester could sense my fatigue.

"It's okay, sweetie. After lunch, I'll show you to your room, and you can rest." His voice was like honey. I loved him instantly.

"Okay boys," Lester said to the half-dozen men gathered around the table. "Let's make our new volunteer, Saskia, a part of the Pippin House family." Encephalopathy. AIDS dementia complex. ADC. Kaposi's sarcoma. Cryptococcal meningitis, toxoplasmosis, PCP. AIDS-related opportunistic infections. My exposure to the new vocabulary was swift and overwhelming.

Almost as overwhelming as my sudden exposure to a world of unfiltered, raw conversation.

"And Ms. Merlot doesn't like pussy," said Gaylord, a handsome young man with red lesions scarring his face. I blushed.

"Nope, young Black cock is more her thing, ain't that right, Ms. Merlot, you fairy queen." Ed (*Marlena?*) grunted at Gaylord. I was so confused.

"Behave yourself, Gaylord," scolded an older gray-haired gentleman wearing a lavender smoking jacket and gray huntsman cap. "This young lady is a refined, well-mannered Catholic college girl who doesn't need to be debased by the drivel coming out of your filthy mouth," said Leonard, the default elder of the group. He was in denial that he was dying of AIDS and believed he was at Pippin House as a spiritual mentor to the young, wayward men who had lost their way. He also had a habit of reaching under their bathrobes and fondling their buttocks.

"Hey, girlie, you know that brown leather means you're into scat," Marlena said. I turned to see who he—she?—was speaking to. *What the hell is scat?*

"She means you, Saskia." Shy, giggly George leaned over and whispered in my ear that in the leather community, brown leather meant being into sex play with "you know, scat. Um, poop." George turned almost as red as I did. I quickly threw out my favorite weathered brown leather jacket.

"I used to have beautiful teeth," Marlena said with a toothless grin, her demeanor suddenly charming and friendly. "And a gorgeous voice. And beautiful breasts." The men at the table all sighed.

"Ed, quit your bellyaching about what you used to be. Marlena Merlot is gone, and you're dying like the rest of us." Gaylord was not one to mince words.

"Am I supposed to call you Ed or Marlena?" I asked politely.

"I don't want you to talk to me at all, girlie. Ed or Marlena, it don't matter because we're not going to be friends."

"Ed, I think it's time for your nap," Lester interrupted. "You can call him Ed or Marlena. He will answer to both. Ed is his given name, and Marlena Merlot was his drag stage name," Lester explained.

"Well, I'd like to be your friend, Marlena," I said. I sensed that she needed the validation. The recognition of her beauty and worth. I vowed to call her Marlena unless she told me otherwise. And I vowed that even if we weren't great friends, she'd warm up to me somehow.

"I had the most beautiful teeth," she repeated. I quickly got used to the absurd, nonsensical turns of conversation of a brain addled with disease.

"The most beautiful. Pearly white," Lester agreed. The rest of lunch passed without incident. The guys bantered with each other. Marlena's skeleton-thin hands were so shaky from medication that she accepted my help feeding her the rest of the creamed corn that hadn't ended up all over me. After lunch, another volunteer assisted with the dishes, and the guys went back to their rooms or sat in the living room and watched *a* VHS. Lester owned a huge movie collection, and there was always something playing. Gaylord was addicted to *Steel Magnolias*. He was often the one to pick the movie.

"I'm going to be the next to die," Gaylord announced in a matter-of-fact tone. "And in heaven, I hope to be doing more than just watching movies, if you catch my drift. So, I'm getting my Shirley MacLaine fix now." The men talked about death as if it were an everyday, normal occurrence. I'd read the accounts of the way in which AIDS was ravaging the gay community, but it hadn't registered. I looked around me at the strangers I would spend the next several weeks with. How many would still be around when it came time for me to head back to campus?

"Everyone here is dying?" I asked Lester.

"Everyone here is living," Lester corrected me. "They are facing death, yes, but so are we all. They just know how they're going to die. And that death will come for them sooner than for you and me."

Once the guys had settled in with popcorn or Ensure, and Lester put Marlena to bed, he showed me to my room. It was small, with a twin bed and a nightstand. A lamp with a rainbow shade was plugged into the wall next to the bed. Collages covered the walls. In the portraits within those collages, some wore silly grins, some had oxygen tubes in their noses, and others were dressed in drag or black leather gear. They all looked happy, at peace.

"They're pictures of the men who've died at Pippin House," Lester explained when he saw me looking. "I consider them guardian angels," he said. "But if it freaks you out, I can move you to another room." I shook my head. No, here with the guardian angels was the perfect place for me to sleep.

"I'm sorry for what you're going through, Saskia. Father Hamilton filled me in," Lester said. "I've got great big shoulders for crying on, and these gigantic ears here can hold a lot of pain." Lester's eyes were green. And kind. I longed to bury my head on his shoulder. At that moment, I knew Lester had been told the real reason I was at Pippin House. I wasn't just a volunteer needing credit for an "immersion experience" in community outreach. I could see in his eyes that he recognized I'd been discarded. No longer an exemplary student worthy of representing campus ministry, I was tainted. And before I could taint the star seminarian, I needed to disappear.

"This room will be perfect. Thank you, Lester."

"Well, that settles that. Let me show you around the rest of the place," he said. "We don't ever call them patients," Lester had explained as he showed me around the home he and his partner Gordon had turned into a hospice. Gordon had died the year before.

The two had been best friends and lovers since their teens. Both had been disowned by their families for being gay. Both HIV positive. They gave up nursing careers with a large local hospital to take in men with AIDS whose families had discarded them.

"As I was saying, we don't call them patients. We're their chosen family. This is their home too. And we bring them home for a chance to live happily and be accepted—while they die." Lester reached out and wrapped his arms around me. "And you're family here too, ladybug." A chill ran through me.

"I collect ladybugs," I said, remembering all the times I had chosen a hand-carved ladybug from Magdalena's after I'd swept the flower shop.

"It's going to be great having someone around full-time," Lester said. "Most of our volunteers are here for an hour or two. Sometimes it's more trouble than help, really. I'll really be able to focus on some projects I've been wanting to get done while you're here," Lester rambled on. "And I'd most like your help with Ed. He's a lost soul and could use a friend, especially as his light in this world is coming to an end." Lester grabbed me in another of his bear hugs I would come to cherish.

"And," he continued, "I imagine you could use a friend as you mourn the soul that you've lost." I felt a tugging at my womb. I don't know how to mourn him. Or whether I'm entitled to the peace of mourning and healing. As a Catholic, I'd memorized a litany of saints, but it wasn't until I met Lester that I believed in angels.

CHAPTER 18

May 1990, Pippin House

WALKING INTO MARLENA'S room was like simultaneously walking into a nursing home, Grateful Dead concert, and crowded men's room at a bar on New Year's Eve. The sickly smell of Vicks VapoRub mingled with vomit, piss, and more than a hint of weed. No matter how many times I stepped into that space, the smell assaulted me, and I had to stifle my gag reflex. Marlena must have seen me wrinkle my nose.

"Ah, the crazy rich White straight girl is offended by my perfume. Eau de AIDS isn't your fragrance?" she teased.

"I prefer Eau de Montezuma's Revenge," I quipped.

She was in a good mood today. Wasn't going to kick me out or tell me to go fuck myself. I relaxed and sat in the wooden folding chair next to her hospital bed. There were few personal touches in her room. The others decorated their spaces—with family photos, art, plants—but Marlena's space was plain. I made a mental note to ask her about that sometime.

Marlena was singing a tune I didn't recognize. Her dachshund Charlie looked up at her from underneath her sweatshirt with his big brown eyes then breathed a deep sigh and snuggled back into his dog nap. "He loves when I sing Dylan. Our favorite crooner,"

Marlena explained. "It's called 'Soon After Midnight.'"

Marlena continued singing in a husky, sultry voice. If I closed my eyes, I could picture her as the magnificent Marlena Merlot in all her shimmery, glittery finery. Charlie's tail started to wag.

As Marlena came to the chorus, Charlie's tail was going so fast now, I worried he'd propel Marlena off the hospital bed.

"'Soon After Midnight'" inspired my drag look," Marlena said. "I imagine that someday I will meet the Fairy Queen on the other side, and I want to be radiant for her."

"Never heard it," I admitted. Marlena beckoned for me to join her on the hospital bed.

"Remember how much I hated you when you got here?" As if I could possibly forget.

The creamed-corn-Ensure mess on my lap. The refusal to take her medicine if I sat next to her at the table. Her obnoxious comments and insistence that I smelled bad.

"I gag every time she walks into the room," Marlena told Lester. "It's like I'm allergic to her pheromones. I'll die sooner if you let her keep volunteering here," she insisted. Lester reminded me again that the disease played funny tricks on Marlena's mind, and sometimes the medications had strange side effects. I shrugged it off. But her words stung. Of course they had. I was clinging to the guys at Pippin House. They kept me from thinking about why I was really there. But somehow, it seemed that Marlena could smell right through me. Like she knew I had a secret and was going to ferret it out at all costs.

"It feels like I've known you all my life," I said. Time had lost its meaning for me. Time was compressed for the dying. Each moment an eternity that dissolved in the blink of an eye.

We sat together in silence for a few moments. Lost in the tenderness of the moment. Aware of the new intimacy, feeling its sweetness, and knowing its brevity.

"Never heard Bob Dylan," she said, shaking her head.

"Of course I've heard Bob Dylan, just not that song."

"Girl, you need an education." She slowly scooted to the far side of the bed and patted the mattress. An invitation.

"Are you sure, Ed?" We'd been making strides, but she still hadn't allowed me to hug her. "I'm sorry, I mean Marlena." I was still adjusting to seeing a man's face and recognizing this didn't necessarily mean male pronouns or names.

"Come over and sit down with me, girlie. But don't let me hear you call me Ed again. That straight-boy name died a long time ago," she said. *What is it with people calling me girlie? First Mike Donohue. Now Marlena.*

"It's a deal. But you have to stop calling me 'girlie' or 'that crazy rich White straight girl,'" I responded. "I'm not rich. And I'm not straight." Marlena's eyes widened in surprise.

"We've got a lot to talk about," she said as I hopped beside her onto the bed. She handed me one strand of her earphones. "But first, Bob Dylan and the Fairy Queen."

We fell into a routine. Every afternoon after Marlena's nap, I'd come into the room, and she'd pat the spot next to her. I'd hop up on the bed, and Charlie would lick my face. And my education would resume. Some days, she wanted to teach me how to be queer. I learned about bears and cubs, otters and twinks. Many of her lessons made me blush. Other days, she wanted to watch old movies—*From Here to Eternity, Sunset Boulevard, Cat on a Hot Tin Roof*. We settled in, and she handed me a joint.

"What am I supposed to do with this?" I asked. I realized how naive I sounded as soon as it came out of my mouth. "Um, I mean, should I be taking your medicinal stuff?"

"Sassy, loosen up. You're too uptight. And we're about to watch the best goddamn queer movie of all time. And you can't fully appreciate it unless you are high." *Sassy. I like it. A nickname. A sign of affection.* That was the first of many trips to Transylvania. To this day, I can't watch *The Rocky Horror Picture Show* without thinking of Marlena and the way we'd cuddle together on that hospital bed, Charlie tucked in her sweatshirt, and the waft of weed. Eau de Contentment.

CHAPTER 19

Early May 1990, Pippin House

ALONG WITH THE antiseptic and putrid smells, death approaching looks like Charlie curled up inside the same ratty gray sweatshirt, breathing warmth onto Marlena's body. It hurts like the ribs that poked my side when I lay down next to her ninety-pound body in the hospital bed. And it sounded like *The Rocky Horror Picture Show*.

"I used to be beautiful in drag," she boasted. Over and over again.

"You're beautiful to me now," I whispered. Because she was. I rubbed her thin, translucent chest with Vicks, careful to avoid lesions. It calmed her, and she sang, "*I'm a sweet transvestite from Transylvania.*" I imagine she once had a deep, sultry voice. Now it was just weak and squeaky.

I remember the first time I touched her skin. Lester had told me I could use gloves if it made me more comfortable. But that had seemed too impersonal. The voices in my head that warned me about catching AIDS were replaced with knowledge of how the virus was actually transmitted. Now I loved touching her. Knowing that such a simple thing, the willingness to touch her, made her feel normal, lovable.

"Beautiful, like Marlena Dietrich." She coughed and took a puff on her joint. "Did I tell you I used to be beautiful in drag?" she asked. "I looked like Marlena Dietrich and sang like her too." Marlena hummed and whispered to Charlie, "Remember me when I die, you rascal." *How could he possibly forget you? And what am I going to do without you?*

"You're beautiful now, my friend." So beautiful.

◆◆◆

Gaylord had been right. He died first. One morning, I headed to the table for breakfast, and his spot sat empty.

"He left us last night," Lester explained. George and Leonard continued to eat as though it was any other day. Marlena was subdued but let me feed her.

"You can help me clean out his room today, Saskia." There wasn't much in Gaylord's room. Some clothes that Lester would donate to Goodwill. There were a few photographs.

"I will try to contact the family to see if they want any of the belongings. But usually by the time they end up in a place like this, there's either no family left to notify, or the family doesn't even acknowledge their death. I keep the photographs in an album," Lester said. "I like to go through them every now and again."

I started to cry. Lester wrapped his arms around me and squeezed. "Honey, it's part of life. I was with Gaylord when he died last night. He had the sweetest smile on his face. He felt no pain. He was ready to be with his lifelong partner who died last year," Lester said.

I wasn't just crying for Gaylord. I was crying for Mama, Opa. For Max, who I never even got to meet. I wanted so desperately to believe they were all together now.

"Do you really believe there's life after death?" I asked Lester.

He nodded. "Yes, I do," he answered. "I'll continue to believe it until I have proof otherwise." We finished cleaning Gaylord's room in companionable silence. The simple act of folding sheets calmed my mind and lifted my spirits.

"I hope so," I said finally. "I mean, I hope there's life after death. I want to meet Max someday."

CHAPTER 20

May 1990, Pippin House

"GET OUT!" SHE screamed with a vitriol directed at me that I hadn't seen since the Ensure and creamed corn incident. The roar that came out of her frail body filled the room and seized my heart with terror. "And don't come back," she whimpered, falling back against the sweat-soaked pillow.

"Stop pretending we're friends," she hissed as I headed toward the door. She breathed a forlorn sigh, and Charlie slid under the collar of her sweatshirt. "You're just nice to me because you have to be." Marlena rolled over on her side, Charlie squirming to accommodate the movement.

"I don't have to be nice to you. Or spend time with you. Or give a shit about you," I said. "I choose to because I love you, whether you believe it or not."

This disease was cruel and destructive and could take control of a person—body, mind, and spirit. Marlena wasn't in control of her rage. And as much as death was expected at Pippin House, when it did strike, it came as an electric shock. Gaylord's room had already been filled; the waiting list for a room grew longer by the day.

I was careful now with my actions. Each one potentially the last. Much as I wanted to slam the door, I closed it gently behind me. Just in case.

―――

I went back to my room and laid down for a nap. I knew I shouldn't take Marlena's words to heart. Her words came out of grief and pain and disease. But they stung. How could I convince her I didn't have to be her friend, that I wasn't pretending? In just a few short weeks, the guys at Pippin House had become my family.

Lester became like a brother to me. To think that any of them thought I was just a volunteer who didn't really care broke my heart. But especially Marlena. Because I did love her, and she was my family. I closed my eyes and was in a deep sleep in a few minutes. Once again, I stood at the edge of a wide field of daffodils. Max cried out to me, but this time was different. The daffodils were fully alive and in bloom, and Max was happy. I reached down and picked him up in my arms. He giggled. "I love you, Mama," he whispered in my ear. "I'll take care of Marlena when she gets here," he said. "She'll love it. It's so much fun. And the Fairy Queen is so beautiful. And so nice. Like you, Mama. Beautiful and nice."

I woke up cradling a tear-stained pillow. I knew it had just been a dream, but for now, I was grateful for the thin veil between this world and the dream world.

―――

Marlena was repeating herself more and more now. Talking about her days as a drag queen. And sometimes talking about her family. She talked about her mom and dad with a pained look on her face.

"Maybe if we got married," she mused, "they would finally forgive me. Married to a beautiful girl. They'd be proud of that." It was a fantasy she brought up over and over again. Marrying me and taking me to meet her family. As good old straight Ed and his fiancé. The life they had dreamed of for their only son. Their only child. "Maybe that way, my parents will love me again. If I'm married to a woman, you know." I didn't make any promises, but I didn't belittle her daydreams either.

"You'll be so handsome in your tuxedo, and I'll wear a lacy white gown and a veil to cover my face," I said. A fantasy. We both knew it. But if it was a fantasy that brought her some peace and comfort, it was one I was willing to indulge.

"You won't ever leave me, will you?" Marlena asked.

"Never, my love. We're family."

CHAPTER 21

Early May 1990, Pippin House

MARLENA'S ROOM SMELLED of antiseptic and sorrow. The letter had come back to her, a yellow RETURN TO SENDER sticker posted on the front envelope. Scrawled across the back, in angry bursts of black marker: YOU ARE A STRANGER TO US. KAREN AND JOHN.

She handed it to me with trembling hands. Not an apology for her outburst but an explanation. That was all I needed.

"Karen and John. They couldn't even sign it Mom and Dad." We sat in silence for several minutes. Marlena held my hand. Her sobs had settled into the occasional shutter and a tear plopping onto the pillow.

"Will you take me to them, please?" she asked. I started to tell her it was a bad idea, but she launched into what must have been a well-rehearsed plea.

"It's just a two-hour drive. We've been talking about taking a road trip anyway. The weather is beautiful, and I'm not going to have many more days outside the house. We can take the mixtape we made, talk, and . . ." All the talking had exhausted her. "And they can't turn me away in person, can they?" Her words trailed off. She knew it was a long shot.

"Marlena, it won't make any difference. Their hearts are full of hate. Seeing you won't change that. If anything . . ." My voice trailed off. She didn't need me to continue.

"If anything," she said, "they'll see me in this dying body, and it will confirm they've been right all along. This is God's punishment for my so-called perversion." She laughed.

"God's a cruel motherfucker," I murmured.

But we prepared for a road trip anyway. As much as Lester agreed with me that it was probably a terrible idea, he believed Marlena deserved to at least try. She was not going to stop begging, and, worse, she was getting more agitated. The more we argued with her, the more Ensure and creamed corn ended up in our laps.

"Just take her on this one last trip, Saskia," Lester said. "She's looking for a particular kind of closure. And she may not get it. But we have to let her try. Let her close this chapter."

"But she really believes that if her parents just physically *see* her, they'll change their minds. She's so convinced that Karen's mother instinct will kick in, and there will be a reconciliation. She's adamant that if her mother is just able to touch the child she brought into the world, she'll soften and see the baby she once held in her arms. And you know that's not going to happen." I was rambling at this point. I knew it was futile to argue. And we all knew that I wasn't going to deny Marlena this last wish.

"You're probably right—maybe even definitely right—but what she will have is an adventure with you, her friend. You'll be there to provide the net if she falls. More likely, though, some time on the open road, seeing the landscape and feeling the wind in her face, will let her forget, just for a moment, that she's about to die."

And so, preparations began. We had diapers in case of an accident. Ensure in case she got hungry. We had extra pillows for the front seat of Lester's Buick so she'd be as comfortable as possible. It was amazing the effort it took to make a dying person's last road trip seem like just another trip around the block.

It occurred to me, as Lester went into the garage to pull the car out, that I didn't feel the emptiness in my womb that had been a continual reminder. A soft ache, but not the heavy emptiness that had settled in. Lester came into the living room and handed me the keys.

"You're all set," he said.

We got fifty miles down the road before Marlena said, "Please stop now." I pulled over to the side of the road.

"I only have one more show in me," Marlena whispered. I knew from the faraway look in her eyes that she was not in the present. "Help me with my hair and makeup and my dress?" I gripped a pretend makeup brush in my hands and gently touched up her face.

"You don't need much, Marlena," I said. "You look so much like Ms. Dietrich, only so much more beautiful." She smiled and rocked back and forth in the passenger seat.

"Are there a lot of people here?" she asked. "Make sure to take a picture of me in this emerald gown." I snapped her photograph and assured her there were hundreds of people waiting to hear her perform.

"Do you hear all that applause?" I asked. "They've just announced your name, and the crowd is desperate to see you and hear you." Marlena shifted in the seat, sat up straight and tall. In her mind's eye, she was on stage, wearing the sequined emerald gown. Her hair and makeup were perfect. She was in good form.

"Do you see my mom and dad in the audience?" I nodded my head.

And she opened her mouth to sing. I couldn't make out the words. Her voice was too weak for even a whisper. She swayed to a

Marlena Dietrich song playing in her head. *I wish I could have seen you perform. You must have been marvelous.*

———◆◆◆———

"Where are we?" Marlena asked. She looked around, bewildered. I reached for her hand.

"We only made it about fifty miles from Pippin House. You asked me to stop driving."

Marlena grinned. "Oh yes, my last show. I was sensational, wasn't I?"

"Sensational," I agreed. "Now, do you want to keep driving or turn around and go home?"

For a moment, I thought she hadn't heard me. When she finally responded, I knew she was grounded in reality.

"Let's go home. I don't need to see them. You're my family now. And Charlie. I want to get home to Charlie." We drove the rest of the way in silence. She'd gotten everything she needed from the trip. And so had I. Marlena would be able to die in peace.

And I'd be able to go on living . . . at peace.

CHAPTER 22

Soon After Midnight, May 13, 1990, Pippin House

"Today would have been Opa's seventieth birthday," I told Marlena. She ignored me.

"Help me clean up this mess. And make sure my going home gown is in tip-top shape," she demanded.

"You're not going anywhere, Marlena," I whispered. But she was ready to go.

"It's getting close to midnight," Marlena said. It was fifteen minutes to the bewitching hour. "I've got a date with the fairy drag queen. I don't want to keep her waiting. And don't forget to play "Soon After Midnight" at my funeral. I promised her I would.

"I'd like to see you off on your date, Marlena. Will you let me?" Marlena motioned for me to take a spot beside her on the hospital bed.

"Say hi to the Fairy Queen for me?" I asked. Marlena nodded. Her breathing was becoming more shallow, more irregular. She put her head down on the pillow. Charlie was tucked in the old, ratty, gray sweatshirt, keeping Marlena warm. "And take care of Max for me?" I asked.

She nodded. "I'll be his fairy godmother," she promised. I lay down and wrapped my arms around her, my head on her shoulder.

She closed her eyes and started to snore softly. And I closed my eyes.

Somewhere between happily and horribly ever after, Marlena died peacefully in her sleep. The smell of Vicks VapoRub and weed wafted in the air. Charlie was tucked underneath the sweatshirt, asleep on Marlena's chest. When she drew her last breath, he let out a tiny whimper.

Sweet forever dreams, my friend. Say hello to the Fairy Drag Queen for me. Somewhere, you are wearing your angel wings and holding your godson, my son Max, in your arms.

I slipped out of the bed and kissed her cheek.

Charlie came over and licked the tears running down my cheeks. Too soon after midnight. Too soon . . .

EPILOGUE

July 1994, Home

MY HAND TREMBLED to get the stick positioned so my piss would hit it. Wendy was hovering over my shoulder. I felt Opa and Mama close by. Felt their joy.

"What does it say? Can you see the cross?" I could feel her breath on my neck and wanted to simultaneously pull her toward me and kiss her nose and push her away so I could concentrate.

"For fuck's sake, Wendy. Chill. I can't pee with you breathing down my neck. Go feed Charlie." Charlie was a bit more arthritic now, but he loved to curl up against my chest, underneath Marlena's raggedy old sweatshirt. Wendy hated the sweatshirt.

"That old rag makes you about as sexy as a fire hydrant," she'd said. I laughed. She had brought laughter back to my life.

But she understood too. Charlie had wandered around, lost in a fog when Marlena died. He wasn't comforted by anyone except me. In truth, I needed that dog as much as he needed me.

I met Wendy at Pippin House. After I graduated from college, I returned there to volunteer. Wendy's brother Adam was a new resident at the house.

"You know, the two of you should just go for it," Adam had said. "I see the way you look at my sister. She likes you too."

The guardian angels of Pippin House continued to watch over me.

◆◆◆

I was in our bathroom. In the home I shared with my girlfriend. *Do you hear that, Marlena Merlot? My girlfriend!* We'd been trying to get pregnant for a while. We finally used a turkey baster filled with the sperm of Adam's straight best friend. Life is so random. Perched on the toilet, I looked around our bathroom. It was a far cry from the dorm bathroom stall. No "Jesus Is Watching You" scratched into the door. Just an adoring partner who was shaking as much as me.

"What does it say?" Wendy squealed. I glanced at the stick quivering like a leaf in my hand.

"It says that Charlie's going to be an uncle." While the two of us danced up and down, Charlie's tail wagged back and forth.

Marlena Otto Nash was born on February 15, 1995, to two adoring moms, a tolerant dachshund, her grandpa Jack, and all the angels and saints, Petra and Otto and a fairy godmother named Marlena.

It was a beautiful, sunny, cold morning when we brought Marlena home. The air tinged with the promise of things to come—her first smile, her first words. *Would she call us Mama and Mommy? Maybe Mutti?* I looked at her perfect angel face and the perfect woman holding her. Home.

Though the grass was tinged with frost and we could see our breath in the air, three daffodils bloomed by the magnolia tree we'd planted in memory of all who had gone before us: Petra, Otto, Max, Lester, Marlena . . .

A litany of saints watching over us.

ACKNOWLEDGMENTS

I want to thank everyone. I feel like the actors on stage accepting their Oscars giving shout-outs while their time to speak is running out. I hate to start listing people because I'm afraid I'll leave someone out. If you're that someone, I thank you here. This book would not have been possible but for the support of the following:

—The Agile Writers' writing community who provided structure, support, and gentle criticism, particularly Greg Smith, whose techy brain created a method for getting the words on the page and my AW critique group, Rishonda Anthony and Whitney Hill.

—René Genese Smith and the crew at the Starbucks at Broad & Bowe, which was a casualty of the 2020 riots in Richmond, Virginia. You provided a safe space for me to write and some really "truth is stranger than fiction" moments.

—Valley Haggard and "Life in 10 Minutes." The first three chapters of *A Date with the Fairy Drag Queen* started as three ten-minute pieces during a writing workshop.

—James River Writers Conference and the Agent Dating Game and the agents who turned down the chance to represent me but who encouraged me to keep going and that my work was "very accomplished."

—To my initial editor, Cindy Cunninham, and Miranda Dillon with Koehler Books. Your expertise made this a much tighter book.

—The Wellspring Writing Collective for inspiring workshops and rejuvenating retreats.

—For old friends (Nicole Sucre) who knew I could do it all along and for new friends (Becky Premock) who now cheer me on.

—And all the men I was honored to know at Horizon House. Especially Chris, the inspiration for Marlena Merlot. May your memories be for a blessing. And to Harry, the inspiration for "Lester," who continues to run Horizon House to this day, I learned more about life in my short time with you than all the book learning I accumulated over many years.

AUTHOR'S NOTE

This is a work of fiction. You might wonder if Saskia is me. While drawn from some real-life experiences, Saskia's story is heavily embellished or made up entirely. Unlike Saskia, my mom is very much alive and has been a huge champion of my writing. Unlike Saskia, I do not hate peanut butter. But we both share a distaste for pumpkin pie.

My opa did not possess magical abilities, yet my relationship with him felt magical. Locations are intentionally vague. I did not live on the East Coast until my late twenties, and Magdalena's Flower Shop doesn't exist, but the *Herrenstrasse* does.

Marlena Merlot is a composite of the beautiful men I was privileged to serve as a volunteer at a home for men dying of AIDS.

This is not a factual record, but that doesn't mean it does not contain nuggets of truth. After all, we do all look at the same moon no matter how far apart we are.

www.ingramcontent.com/pod-product-compliance
Lightning Source LLC
LaVergne TN
LVHW041610070526
838199LV00052B/3078